MW00953391

THE FALL of

MARS

LUKAS JAGLOWSKI

Copyright © 2019 Lukas Jaglowski

Written by Lukas Jaglowski

 @LukeJaglowski

Edited by Melissa J. Hayes

Hayes Editorial Services

Cover art by Sinead Treacy

 @sidoopa

ISBN: 978-1-0891-2789-5

In loving memory of Spirit & Opportunity

2003-2010

2003-2018

This story was inspired by your discoveries

ATTENTION:

While we are being forced to remain anonymous, this is an important message, from a credible source.

The following is a copy of the recovered journal of Adam Jelani. The original was found by an archaeologist at an excavation site in Somaliland, Somalia. This volume has been translated from its original language—apparently similar to the writings of ancient Greece—into modern English. Using stratigraphy, we have estimated the journal to be roughly 200,000 years old. The ancient Greek empire was only about 2,500 years ago, which obviously makes this journal a fascinating, yet puzzling, find. The journal itself was inside a box made out of some kind of metal, nothing we would expect to be here 200,000 years ago.

It seemed obvious to us that we must have made a mistake, so we were shocked when several other archaeological teams confirmed the same findings. Based on how deep the metal box was found in the ground, it had to have been put there sometime between 190,000 and 210,000 years ago.

Not too long after the translation was completed, the original journal went missing. It was unclear whether it had been stolen, destroyed, or simply lost.

We understand how hard this is to believe, but that doesn't matter. The truth will remain the truth for all eternity. You may choose to believe us, or you may not. Nonetheless, everything you are about to read is real.

Chapter One
ME AGAINST THE WORLD

08/06/15AX

I don't know how to start this. I've never kept a journal before. I guess I should probably introduce myself.

My name is Adam Jelani. I'm twelve Mars years old, and I work for the Martian International Project of Exploration (or, simply, MIPE), as a robot operator in their casting department. Well, that's what my résumé says, anyway. I haven't done that in about a year. Technically, I guess you could say I'm a drug dealer.

About a year ago, King Xavier shut down MIPE because he said it was a waste of funds. MIPE was the space program for Mars. It was actually pretty cool. We built ships designed for going into outer space and landing on the moons, then returning. The program did that for twenty-five years, and it was just starting to look into the idea of finally going to another planet in our solar system. The planet that made the most sense for us to visit was Gaia. The reason was simple: It was close to us, and we had enough evidence that the planet could host life.

Gaia looks a lot like Mars; the land is just shaped differently. Where Mars has one big piece of land on the south, with one big ocean on the north, Gaia has several pieces of land, with the ocean surrounding them all. We can see a lot of green areas on the land, which obviously is plant life; there has to be animal life, as well.

We started designing the ship that was supposed to go to Gaia; well, the engineers did. When they finally thought it was ready, they had us make the parts for a prototype. When it was finally done, they did some tests on it, and I guess they liked it, because they had us make a lot more parts.

Then, one day, while I was running my robots, there was a fire drill. Once everyone was out, they told us all to go home. The fire department never even showed up or anything; it was like they were trying to get us out as quickly as possible.

The next day I showed up to work, and the building was surrounded by the Martian Army. I tried to drive in, but I was stopped by a soldier who came up to my window. I quickly said, "It's okay—I work here."

He responded with, "Not anymore. No one works here now."

I was confused, but drove back home and called my boss. He said they had told him the same thing.

I didn't used to think much about it; places go out of business all the time. But now it's been just over a year, and this place is still being guarded like it's a secret base. If the program was really shut down due to a waste of funds, why wouldn't they just sell everything left in the building and use it for something else? They are paying these soldiers more to guard the building than what they were paying us to work there, from what I've heard.

So, anyway . . . I'm about to attempt something incredibly insane, or maybe incredibly genius. I haven't figured out which it is yet. And in the likely event that I don't succeed, I want my attempts to be documented in some way. That's what this journal is for.

I'm going to Gaia. I don't really know how, but I am; or I will die trying. We know there has to be life there, so why won't they send off the ship we already made to see what's there?

The only idea that makes any sense is that King Xavier knows what is on Gaia and he doesn't want the public to find out. Call me a conspiracy theorist or whatever, but you can't tell me that shit isn't suspicious. So, I'm gonna go find out.

I am aware I could die, but stepping foot on Gaia has always been a dream of mine since I was a kid. This is the only way I'll ever get to do it.

I will write everything I know in this journal. If I don't succeed, maybe someday, someone will find it and take over where I left off.

09/06/15AX

I've realized I can't do this by myself. I will need some people who are willing to do something this crazy with me. I don't really know who; I don't talk to many people because I don't like many people. The only person I can think of to ask is my friend Bahaadur Hades, and that's it. I usually just call him Hades, because I think his first name is too hard to say. Hopefully, he knows other people who might be interested and can be trusted.

He and I have been working on smuggling drugs since the shutdown of MIPE, mostly kratos and asclepius, to Martian military members. If you don't know what those two things are, kratos is an addictive powder that some people sniff to feel more powerful. Asclepius is a green flowering plant that is smoked by pretty much everyone, yet is somehow still illegal.

I get the stuff, and he delivers it to sixteen different people in both the army and the navy. Then, they distribute it to everyone else. So Hades has a lot more contact with people than I do.

I will talk to him tomorrow about this idea, and hopefully he will take it seriously.

10/06/15AX

I talked to Hades today. I had him come over to my shitty apartment for a few joints and beers. I told him my idea and he thought I was just really high, talking crazy. He wasn't taking it seriously at all.

"Oh, you're gonna go to Gaia, just like that?" he said sarcastically.

"Well, no. That's why I came to you. I'll need help," I replied.

"What am I gonna do to help? Throw you there?" he said, laughing.

"Can you be serious for a second?" I asked impatiently.

Hades laughed again, finally saying, "Fine. What do you need me to do?"

"I need someone with eyes inside the MIPE building. One of the guards," I explained.

"Just any guard? There's a lot."

"One we can trust."

Hades thought about it for a second and said, "There's only one I trust."

"Okay, who?" I asked.

"Sergeant Jack Zelus," he replied. "But everyone just calls him Z."

Hades called Z and set up a time for the next day, when we could sit down and have a talk with him, right after he gets off his shift at the MIPE building.

13/06/15AX

Hades introduced me to Z today.

We met at a diner in Lynesburg. Z walked in singing along to music he was listening to on his headphones. He's about my height, a year or two older. He looks like the typical Martian Army soldier, bald and pretty well-built.

There wasn't anyone else in the diner other than the employees. I guess it was just a slow day.

We took a seat at a booth, and Z took off his headphones. We shook hands.

"This is Adam, the guy I was telling you about," said Hades. "And Adam, this is—"

"Okay," Z interrupted. "I know he's Adam, and he knows I'm Z. I don't got a lot of time; I gotta watch my show. What do you need?"

"Well, I need your help with something," I said.

"No shit. Get to the point," Z replied impatiently.

"I need you to help me steal a Martian spacecraft."

He kinda laughed and then slowly went back to a straight face.

"Wait . . . are you serious?" he asked. "Is that even possible?"

"Well, I was hoping you would know if it was or not."

"I can get you in the door," he said. "As far as stealing a fuckin' spacecraft goes, that's on you to figure out. But even getting you in the door is pretty risky. There would have to be something in it for me. Whaddya got to offer?"

"Peace. A life where you do more than guard buildings," I said.

"Well, that sounds great," Z said with a smile, "but I'd need something a little more guaranteed."

Before I could respond, Hades tossed a bag containing about seven grams of kratos to Z. I don't know why he had to do it out in the open like that. There wasn't anyone around, but still. The Martian Army has been cracking down on that shit a lot lately.

I guess it worked, though. Z looked at the bag and said, "Well, you're gonna need Martian Army uniforms. Even if I can get you in the door, you will definitely get stopped before you get close to the hangar. You need to blend in." Z scowled, then said, "The next problem is, you two don't look like military men at all."

He was right. Members of the Martian military are usually in very good shape, because of their incredibly strict training. Although I don't get what the point of all the training is. Ever since King Maxwell united all nations of Mars in the year 347 (seventeen years before King Xavier restarted the calendar), there hasn't been a single war. The Martian military has no one to fight except for its own.

Army men typically work as police officers, or as guards at prisons and off-limit sites, like the MIPE building. The navy is slightly more active, patrolling the ocean all day to try to prevent piracy, which has become pretty common lately.

Anyway, Hades is pretty huge, and not in a muscular way. He also has tattoos just about everywhere, including his face—not your typical soldier. As for me, I'm just not in the right kind of shape; I don't have the amount of unnecessary muscle the average soldier has. Plus, my hair is a little grown out. Soldiers are always either bald or buzzed. Z said he will help us, but that we need to work on a better plan if we want this to actually work.

14/06/15AX

Okay, after a long night of discussions between Hades and me, we have somewhat of a plan now. Hades could easily hide his face and hand tattoos with makeup, and the rest would be covered by clothing. Also, even considering his weight, he could still pass for a Martian Navy commodore. He would have to go in alone, because I wouldn't pass for a commodore, but he seemed to be okay with that. We believe it's a great idea, but Z had some concerns.

"Commodore?! Look—you guys want me to get you two soldier's uniforms, that's no biggie. But there's no commodore uniforms just lying around. People have to earn that shit."

Hades quickly responded by saying he'd double the pay.

Z sighed before saying, "I guess I'll see what I can do."

I had no idea why Hades was willing to give up half an ounce of kratos for my plan, but I didn't ask.

18/06/15AX

It's been four days, but Z finally supplied us with the uniform today. We met at the same diner as last time. Z gave us the backpack with Hades' uniform inside, then said, "We good? You need anything else?"

"We need another man," I replied. "A pilot. You know any? Preferably one who doesn't like Xavier."

"A lot of people might say they want to rebel, but most of them are probably just talking out of their asses," Z said.

"But there is one guy I know who might actually hate Xavier enough to do it. Captain Ricardo Eurus. Cool dude."

"Has he ever flown a spacecraft?" I asked.

"Nah, but he passed on a spacecraft simulator."

"Would you be able to tell Captain Eurus about our mission, without the information getting to the wrong people?"

"Of course! If anyone finds out who shouldn't, I'll just kill them," Z said with a smile.

I didn't know if he was kidding or not, but I didn't really care.

19/06/15AX

It was right before sunrise when I woke up to a knock at the door of my shitty apartment.

At first, I had no idea what was going on; it wasn't the most pleasant way to be woken up. As I pulled myself off the uncomfortable couch and walked to the door, my heart sank as I looked out the peephole and saw the Martian Army logo on the man's jacket sleeve.

I didn't know what to do—until I realized the man was by himself and appeared to be unarmed. I thought it might still be a trap of some kind. However, as I looked closer I noticed his name badge. Ricardo Eurus! Sure enough, he was equipped with a captain's badge on his other sleeve. As my panic finally eased, I opened the door.

"Adam Jelani?" the man asked.

"Captain Ricardo Eurus?" I replied.

"Yeah, but just call me Eurus . . . actually, Captain Eurus."

"Of course, Eurus . . . ah, I mean, umm, Captain . . . Eurus." I grew more anxious as Eurus stared at me. Finally, his straight face broke as he began laughing.

"I'm joking. Just call me Eurus." Most members of the Military prefer being called by their last name, since they are forced to refer to each other by last name while on duty.

Eurus was a little shorter than me, but about the same age. He had a scar across the left side of his forehead, about as long as the average male index finger. He was more built than Z and had buzzed hair and a full beard. His eyes were a light blue, which really stood out from his dark skin.

If you're reading this journal in the future and you're not a Martian, all Martians have dark skin and blue eyes. However, the eyes are all different shades of blue. Eurus's eyes are on the lighter side, while mine are a darker shade. There was a point in time when Martians had different skin colors and eye colors, but due to centuries of interracial unions, we've all become one mixed race.

Eurus sat down on the couch I had just awoken from, as there weren't many other places to sit. I awkwardly sat down beside him.

"So, my boy Z said you need a spacecraft pilot, for something against Xavier," Eurus said. "Sounds like my kind of party. Where do we start?"

"Z said you've only flown a simulator," I said. "Are you sure you could fly the real thing?"

"No shit—that's the whole point of the simulator," he said, somewhat defensively. "It's a perfect simulation of flying a real MIPE spacecraft."

"Uh, okay," I said. "Can you get yourself to where the spacecraft are kept and see if there's any way to safely fly one out? Just find them and scope out the area. I need some eyes in there other than Z."

"Yeah, sure," Eurus replied. "But what am I getting out of all this?"

"You can keep the spaceship when we're done."

Eurus thought about it for a second and said, "Okay. So what's the plan?"

"We'll talk tomorrow," I replied. "After you scope out the spaceships in the building."

20/06/15AX

All of us met up today, everyone who knows—Hades, Z, Eurus, and myself. When Eurus woke me up yesterday, I was too tired to recall that I'd never told him where I lived. Apparently that didn't matter, as Z and Eurus informed me today that the Martian Army is able to get all pertinent information on anyone, at any time. So today's meeting was held in my apartment, since they all know where it is now anyway.

Eurus said. "They wouldn't let me up to the top floor. Sorry. I tried to talk my way past the guards, but it wasn't working."

"Wait—guards? But I thought *you* were a guard," I said.

"Yeah, I am," Eurus replied. "But certain areas are guarded by higher-level guards, the shit that even Z and I can't see. I knew that, but thought I could get in anyway, because I know them. But I guess not."

As a former employee of MIPE, I knew that the ships were on the very top floor of the MIPE building. The roof, built during the time of the moon landings, opened up to allow ships to take off from there directly. Rockets would take off from the roof in the middle of the day without disturbing anyone. The building was so tall that if it were a cloudy day, people would have no idea a launch was even happening.

So I asked the group, "Could they be using the ships? And only on cloudy days?"

"What about at night?" asked Hades.

It wasn't impossible. The ships we were designing at MIPE did not have any fuel, or even an engine, unlike the previous ones used for getting to the moons. They only have a small vigor reactor in the center of the ship which powers everything. It does put off light, but it's covered on the ship. It may not be visible at night, and also makes no noise other than a very subtle hum, which would be impossible to hear unless you were close to it. I have seen a prototype, but I've never seen one take off. When they were first demonstrated, I saw one hover inside the building.

How would we find out if they were using them? And why *would* they be? Even if we did find out they were using them, that still wouldn't help us figure out how to get one.

I remembered Hades' commodore uniform.

"Could Hades get past the guards and into a ship if he was wearing the uniform?"

"Probably," answered Z. "They might wonder why they'd never seen him before, but he could be from a different troop somewhere else on the planet, so they probably wouldn't question it. Problem is, he wouldn't know how to fly it."

"Bring your phone," said Eurus, "I'll walk you through takeoff and getting the ship to wherever the rest of us are hiding."

"Are you sure you can do that?" I asked

"It's gonna be my ship when we're done," he replied. "I wouldn't risk it if I wasn't sure."

The mission will take place on 31/06, which is a holiday. It's King Xavier's twenty-fifth birthday. School will be out, and most workers will have the day off.

Z and Eurus informed me that about half the guards also have the day off. Which hopefully makes the mission much easier, Z still has guard duty, which is a good thing, because he's our key in the door. Eurus has the day off—also a good thing. This fits into the plan perfectly, as no one will ask any questions when he doesn't show up.

Z will let Hades in. Hades will casually walk to the elevator and go to the top floor. He will then walk by the officers as they salute him, like all officers do to commodores.

If all goes as planned, no one will say a thing to Hades. He will get on a ship and call Eurus, who will direct him on how to fly out of the building and land on the ground outside, where we'll be waiting. Eurus will take over, and we'll be on our way to Gaia.

30/06/15AX

Tomorrow is the day.

I haven't written at all in recent days because nothing has really happened. We decided on our plan ten days ago; since then, we've all just been mentally preparing ourselves for what is about to happen. We know we might not live past tomorrow, so we have been getting our affairs in order. Saying good-bye to the people in our lives, just in case.

At least, that's what I'm assuming the other three are doing. I don't really have anyone to say good-bye to. And I don't really have any affairs to get in order, since I've been unemployed for a year and have no family.

I've been spending this time thinking of what we are gonna do once we get to Gaia. I've been looking through my old MIPE research, to see what we even know about the planet. We know there is oxygen, and it's closer to the sun, so it will be warmer than we are used to. We know there is water; well, I feel confident about it, anyway. It doesn't say that in the research, but we can see it. They can argue that the blue might not be water, but if we know there is oxygen, then it has to be water, right?

I packed some food and first-aid supplies. We won't really know what is safe to eat and what isn't, so the food I'm bringing should last us until we figure that out.

This may be the last thing I write, but for some reason, I'm sure it won't be.

Tomorrow, right after the sun sets, I will meet up with Z and Eurus at Simba's Field, where they play baseball at the local school, the largest piece of open land near the MIPE building. And we will wait for Hades' call . . .

Chapter Two

NOT AFRAID

31/06/15AX

This is too much. I'm not sure if I should keep doing this. I don't know—whatever; this is what happened.

I met with Eurus at Simba's Field. It was right after sunset, about fifteen minutes after Z had let Hades in the building, just like we'd planned. Z then met up with us to wait for Hades. After about an hour, we finally received a call from him.

"I have no idea where I'm going. I've never been in this building before," Hades said, sounding frustrated.

"It's the top floor," I said. "It's not that complicated; just keep going up."

"I'm scared. What if I get caught?"

I didn't know how to respond right away. What if he *did* get caught? I wouldn't have any idea what to do. But we couldn't be thinking like that, so I thought fast and said, "I'll stay on the phone with you the whole time. If you get caught, I'll know right away, and we will come save you." I had no idea how we would save him if it came to that; I was just saying it to help him calm down.

It was unusual. Hades is the most feared gangster I've ever met, and now he's saying he's scared. It was a sign that maybe this plan was really stupid and we shouldn't be doing it, but I ignored the signs.

I walked Hades through getting to the top floor. When he arrived at the entrance to the spaceport on the very top floor, the fear in his voice grew much heavier. I knew where he was from my experience in the building. He was right outside the large black gate which was usually unlocked—at least it was when I still worked there.

Before Hades was close enough for anyone to hear him, I asked him what he saw. He described the large black gate and said it was open, but that two armed guards were standing on either side.

"Okay . . . just walk past them, through the gate," I said.

"Okay," said Hades, clearly uncertain.

I could hear what was going on through the phone.

"Name, Commodore?" said one voice.

"What?" said Hades, confused.

"Name, sir?"

"Oh . . . Commodore . . . Dolos."

"Why does a commodore need to visit a spacecraft port?" asked one of the guards.

"Uh, research for a . . . a spacecraft carrier," responded Hades.

I was surprised—yet relieved—by how quickly he had thought of a response. We hadn't anticipated that anyone would speak to him, but I guess it was a pretty valid question.

"I'm in," said Hades a few moments later, no longer sounding scared. I guess he'd been more worried about getting past the guards than flying a spaceship.

Hades' voice had changed. Now he sounded amazed, in awe.

"These ships. They're beautiful," he said.

"I know," I responded. "How many are there? There was only one when I left MIPE, but we had a lot of parts to make more."

"There's three. Actually, two. One is leaving right now."

They *are* using them. But why?

"Do you see anything unusual?" I asked.

"Well, I see a spaceship silently taking off through the roof of this building, so yes," he said sarcastically.

"I mean, anything that might help us figure out what they're doing?"

"No . . . I don't really know what I'm looking for. Can I please just get on a ship and get this over with?" Hades was obviously impatient and feeling way too anxious to notice any details that might help.

"Whatever—get in whichever ship is closest," I replied, "but don't make eye contact with anyone."

Once he was safely on the ship, I handed the phone to Eurus.

"All right, my dude. You see the touch screen in front of the captain's seat?" Eurus asked.

"Yeah, I got it," answered Hades.

"All right, slide a finger across it, and it should light up."

"It worked," Hades confirmed.

"Word. Now, the first thing you wanna do is press the 'seal' button. This should tightly seal all openings to the ship, so no one can get in before you take off," Eurus explained. "Once you've done that, press the un-mount button. This will put the craft into hover."

"Don't I have to power it on?" asked Hades.

"It's always powered on. The only thing you need to do to start is un-mount. So press it."

"Okay, I'm in hover," said Hades, "but I hear people outside yelling, and they're trying to talk to me on the radio. I can't really hear what they're saying."

"Who cares what they're saying?" Eurus said. "Shut the radio off so it doesn't distract you. Now, use the touchpad to access the top-view camera; it will show you what is directly above you. Make sure the roof is still open and you have plenty of space."

After a pause, Hades responded, yelling, "It's closing right now! But there's still enough space if I hurry! What do I do?!"

"Okay, okay. On the top of the screen where it says the ship is in hover, there should be something similar to an

Internet search bar. Type in 'forty feet vert–plus' and press 'enter.' It will shoot the ship directly up into the air, forty feet."

"How do you spell 'vert'?" yelled Hades.

"Seriously?"

"I didn't know I was gonna have to spell shit to operate a spaceship!"

"V-E-R-T!" Eurus shouted.

None of us could hear or see what was going on, but Hades said it worked.

"Okay, man. Now open up the tab labeled 'coordinates,' " Eurus continued. "Once it's open, you will notice the ship has your exact coordinates displayed. Under that, there is a bar labeled 'destination coordinates.' This is only used once the ship is already on a planet, like it is now. This feature will not do anything when we're in space. Anyway, type in the coordinates of where Z, Adam, and I are: three degrees, fifteen minutes, forty-two seconds north, seventy-eight degrees, thirty-nine minutes, fifty seconds west. Then, hit 'enter.' The ship will take you to the coordinates by itself."

A few minutes passed, and then we all saw the large, black, saucer-shaped craft float toward the baseball field, defying gravity. As the ship grew closer, we noticed a pair of lights in the distance, behind the ship. The lights approached us a lot faster than the ship did.

As the ship reached the middle of the field, where we'd planned for Hades to land it and pick up the three of us, the two lights arrived at the same time and were now noticeably two Martian Army helifighters.

Z cupped his hands around his mouth and yelled, *"FUCK THE POLICE!!"* directly at them.

"Yo, relax," said Eurus.

"They can't hear me," Z said reassuringly.

The three of us quickly hid in the dugout, watching everything from behind a metal fence. Over one of their loudspeakers we heard, "Return this craft to the MIPE building immediately. You have ten seconds to start moving toward the building or you will be shot down!"

The craft did nothing, just remained there, hovering over the baseball field, with a helifighter on either side.

My phone starting ringing. It was Hades. I immediately put the phone on speaker so Eurus and Z could hear.

"How do I go back? I don't wanna die, man!" yelled Hades, terrified.

Eurus answered quickly. "There's a button on the touch screen! Open up the coordinates tab again and click on where it says 'return to previous coordinates'!"

"Okay, I got it!"

But it was too late. Both helifighters set off one missile each. As the missiles were heading toward the ship, it started to move slowly back toward the building. As the missiles crashed into the ship, the dark baseball field was lit up by the explosion. Everyone's ears were ringing, and no one knew if Hades was okay.

When I saw that the ship was still hovering, but not moving anymore, I tried to call Hades. There was no answer. Each helifighter shot off three more missiles apiece, each exploding against the ship one at a time. We all watched as the burning ship crashed into the baseball field, dirt and shrapnel launching everywhere. The metal fence saved us from the largest pieces of shrapnel, but small bits flew in, cutting Z's left shoulder. As clouds of dust poured down on us, we were all temporarily blinded.

As the dust cleared we all blinked over and over, trying to get the dirt out and regain our vision. I made my way out of the dugout and realized Eurus was already outside. Z followed behind me, putting pressure on his shoulder wound with a T-shirt.

"The helifighters are gone," said Eurus, out of breath. "They probably didn't see us."

"But the ship is in pieces," I said. "There's no way Hades could have survived. And we can't stay and look for him; they're definitely gonna be sending a crew to clean all this up."

It was hard to see much of the debris, it was so dark outside. But I did notice one small light between second and third base. I walked over to it as Eurus checked on Z's wound.

As I approached the light, I realized it was the reactor that powered the ship, approximately the size of my two hands together. I picked it up and hid it under my shirt. Or at least, tried to. The light shone through, making it obvious there was something under there.

As I started to walk back towards Z and Eurus, I was horrified to notice one of Hades' hands in the debris. I could see his tattoos on it and everything, with the cover-up we used melting off. I felt paralyzed, realizing he was really gone.

Eurus yelled to me, "Come on, let's go!" As I snapped out of my paralysis, "Z will be fine once I can clean the wound and put some stitches. . . Wh—what the fuck's under your shirt?"

"The reactor," I replied. "With this, my experience at MIPE, and my leftover research, I can make my own ship."

"Oh, so you're an engineer now?" asked Z. "Don't you think that shit's a little fuckin' noticeable?"

"Let's just get to the car," I said. "I'll put it in the trunk right now before anyone shows up and we'll get out of here."

As we drove toward my apartment, several Martian Army cargo trucks passed us on the street. Luckily, we had already passed by the mall before we passed these trucks, so there was no reason for them to suspect anything.

We arrived safely at my apartment, and instead of going all the way up to the seventy-seventh floor with a stolen, glowing piece of government equipment, we went one floor down, to my storage unit.

It was the middle of the night, so no one else was down there to witness anything. Eurus took Z to the main-floor bathroom, where there is always a first-aid kit, to treat his wound, while I locked the reactor inside the safe in my storage unit. Then, I met the crew outside the bathroom after Eurus was done cleaning and bandaging Z's wound. He even stitched him up with an emergency stitch kit he always keeps on him.

We parted ways for the night, and said we'd start on a new plan tomorrow.

As my head touched the pillow, it started to hit me: My best friend had just died . . . all because he had listened to me and trusted me. I should have known our plan had too many holes in it. I was just so eager to get off this planet, and on Gaia. I should have thought smarter, not faster. I'm sorry, Bahaadur Hades. Rest in peace.

I'm not much of an artist, but I've had this image stuck in my head since it happened, so I figured I'd draw it out. This is the ship over Simba's Field, right before they fired the missiles.

Chapter Three
THIEVES IN THE NIGHT

33/06/15AX

Yesterday, Eurus, Z, and I had a private gathering to mourn Hades' death. We couldn't have a real funeral because no one could know about his death yet. No one could know that we'd had anything to do with the grand theft of a spaceship.

As the three of us passed around a blunt and poured some liquor in honor of Hades, Eurus brought up a very good point.

"You do know we have to finish this now, right?" he said. "Hades' death can't be meaningless. People need to look back and know he died a hero."

He was right.

We'll need supplies. I'll write more later—Eurus just showed up.

34/06/15AX

Eurus and I spent all day and night working on our new plan, knowing that it just has to work; we cannot lose another man.

"What exactly are we gonna need?" Eurus asked while we were eating some pizza I had ordered.

"Well, we need a lot of chazakium, preferably in sheets," I replied. "It's the only metal that can withstand moving at the speed of light without falling apart. It will form the outside of the craft, protecting everything underneath."

"Okay. What else?"

"Most importantly, we need a vigor converter," I said. "It connects the vigor reactor to the spinning shell of the ship, which allows the shell to spin at light speed. This converts the ship into more of an energy than a form of matter. This is what makes the ship ignore the rules of gravity."

"Word."

"Problem is, it might be impossible to find," I said. "I might have to make my own. I should probably start that first, as it will probably be the hardest part."

Although I'd built spaceship shells and chassis before while with MIPE, anything vigor-related had always been handled by a separate department. With that being said, however, during orientation we'd been shown several videos, including one that had explained how a vigor converter works. It's a long shot, and I'll be working off only memory, but I have to try.

"Keep going—I'm making a list on my phone," said Eurus.

"I'll need an RC car, a good one . . . and the highest-powered magnets we can possibly find . . . I need silver, gold, or copper, and some chazakium for the converter itself—but not nearly as much as I'll need the for the ship's shell. We should be able to get the amount we need for the converter at a hardware store."

"Okay. Is that it?" asked Eurus.

"No, I'll need some hydrollion wiring."

"What the fuck?" Eurus said. "I think you're just starting to make shit up."

"No, it's wiring with an outer shell made of an unbreakable, glass-like material, and the inside conductor is a silver-water mixture. It's the only type of wiring that can transport the power of the vigor reactor through the converter and throughout the ship. It starts out flexible, but cannot be used until you harden it. Once the wires are exactly where you want them, you heat them with a lighter or torch and then the wires harden to their unbreakable form."

"Uh, okay."

As Eurus and I went over the list, we realized we needed more money. It may have been wrong of us, but I took Eurus to Hades' old hideout. We found enough cash there to build three ships if we wanted to. I also grabbed some kilos of kratos and asclepius to pay off Z, and to have a little fun when we felt like celebrating. I already had plenty of asclepius, but you can never have enough, right?

Anyway, I'm off to get supplies for this converter. I'm sure there's more stuff I need other than what I've listed, but hopefully it will come to me as I shop. One thing is for certain: I can't build this ship in my shitty apartment.

35/06/15AX

Well, I got all the supplies I'll need, including the things I forgot to add to the list earlier. Like a small foundry oven, about the size of a common stove, which will melt down the metal for me; it actually wasn't as hard to find as I thought it would be. All I had to do was act like a jewelry forger interested in looking for new supplies. I did have to get the highest-powered one, however, since I could only find copper. The oven has to be able to reach at least 1,085 degrees in order to melt that. (While all of the ovens could reach that temp, no problem, I realized I will probably have to melt down the chazakium for some parts of the ship, which melts at 4,200 degrees.) The oven is now in my storage unit, with the reactor.

We'll need a warehouse or garage of some kind. Hades would have been my go-to guy for finding something like that, but he's no longer with us.

I called Z, figuring he might know someplace large enough, or at least know someone who does. I told him to come by my apartment. With everything going on now, we can't ignore the possibility that our phones might be tapped, even though we're still pretty sure no one knows of our plan.

There was a knock at the door, and I assumed it was Z. As I opened the door, I was surprised to see a very frightened Eurus standing there with a huge bruise and gash under his eye.

"They know I was there! They know I was there, man!" he yelled as he ran into the apartment.

"Okay, okay. Chill. What are you talking about?" I asked.

"A Martian Army colonel showed up at my doorstep with two other armed soldiers. They walked right into my house and asked me to take a seat," Eurus explained. "The colonel looked right at me and said, 'What were you doing at Simba's Field on the thirty-first?' I didn't know what to say. I didn't understand how they knew I was there . . ."

"So what *did* you say?" I asked.

"That I didn't know what they were talking about," Eurus replied in a calmer voice. "Don't worry, I played it cool. But somehow they know I was there."

"So they just left? They let you go?"

"Not exactly," Eurus said as he sat on my couch. "They told me they'd be back, and not to leave town unless I plan on an early funeral, or some clichéd bullshit like that. I didn't give them any information, even after one of the soldiers hit me in the face with the butt of his gun several times. But they know I was there."

About this time, Z finally showed up. He was wearing a tank top, his shoulder still wrapped in a bandage. You could see a spot of blood on it where the shrapnel had hit.

"Yo, aren't you ever gonna change that bandage?" asked Eurus.

"Why are you asking about *me*?" Z replied. "Let's talk about what the fuck happened to your face."

Eurus told Z pretty much everything he'd just told me.

"Well, no one showed up at my place," Z said. "How did the army know you were there, but not me?"

"I don't know," said Eurus, "but I can't go back home. I brought all my essentials in a bag, in my car outside. I also can't go back to work, obviously. I guess I'm on the run now."

"We all are," I said. "If they know about one of us, we have to assume they know about all of us. Z, even though no one has confronted you yet, for your safety, and that of the mission, I strongly suggest you don't go back to work either. Go back home and get your stuff. We'll all meet back here tonight. Also, Z, we need a warehouse of some kind— somewhere we can all hide and build this ship, where no one will come looking for us. And a truck so we can load up all the supplies and transport them to the warehouse. Can you do that?"

"Damn, that's a lot," Z replied, "but I can do anything. See you later tonight."

As Z started to walk toward the door, Eurus stopped him.

"Hold up, man. Come over here. Let me put a new bandage on that for you. It's disgusting."

"I can put on my own bandage," Z replied as he turned around. "I just changed it before I made my way over here."

"What?!" exclaimed Eurus. "Did you run into a wall or something?"

"Umm . . . no. Why?" said Z, confused.

"Because it shouldn't be bleeding like that still. Let me look at it, please."

Z sat down by Eurus, waiting for him to put gloves on before removing the bandage.

"Does it hurt?" asked Eurus.

"It's not too bad."

Eurus pushed down on the wound.

"Ahhhhh!! Yo, what the *fuck*!" yelled Z.

"Not too bad, huh?" joked Eurus.

Z remained quiet, trying to appear as tough as possible.

"It looks like it's oozing, but it's . . ."

After an awkward pause, I had to ask. "What?"

"Well, look," answered Eurus. He showed me the wound, which had a weird purple pus coming out of it. "It doesn't make any sense. That doesn't look like anything made by the body. Z, you didn't notice this?"

"I didn't look at it," Z replied. "You really want me to be honest? Wounds that big freak me out. When I change the bandage, I do it with my eyes shut. If I look at it, I might pass out."

Eurus and I laughed. Z looked like he was gonna knock us out, so we tried to quiet our laughter, but it was too damn funny.

"I'm gonna cut the stitches," said Eurus. "The pus is coming out of the wound, so I'll have to look deeper inside it to figure out what it can possibly be from." Eurus put some kratos on the wound to temporarily numb it, then cut the stitches with his knife. As the wound opened, more blood and the strange purple pus poured out, running down Z's arm and onto my wood floor. Eurus tried to soak up some of it with a towel, but it was too late; my floor was already stained with it. (Not that it matters much, as it was already stained from a bunch of other shit anyway.)

As the bleeding calmed down, Eurus looked into the wound. The more he looked, the more confused he appeared.

"I think . . . I think there's something in there," he said.

"Probably a leftover piece of shrapnel," I said.

"Yeah, and it must contain some sort of purple liquid or grease," Eurus said. "That would explain why it hasn't been healing properly; the liquid from the shrapnel wasn't letting it. Here, I'll get it out."

I watched as Eurus used a pair of tweezers to remove the foreign item. It looked like it was made of some sort of metal, in the shape of a small torpedo. It was damaged and broken in half, purple fluid dripping out, with some sort of small wiring inside. It was hard to make out any details with it being so damaged.

"Damn, you had this shit inside your arm?" Eurus asked, handing the object to Z, who examined it.

"Damn, I wonder what part of the ship it came from," said Z. "Must be like a fuse or something."

I've spent a lot of time working on these ships, and that was no fuse. In fact, it was like nothing I'd ever seen used as any part of a spacecraft. It wasn't like anything you'd find at a baseball field, either.

Quietly, as Eurus and Z continued talking, I stood up and walked over to my kitchen table that was covered with supplies for the vigor converter. I grabbed one of the magnets and walked back over to the guys. I put the magnet up to Eurus's left shoulder, the same side as Z's injury. Eurus and Z's conversation came to a halt after they both noticed I was using the magnet to pull Eurus's shoulder. A section of his skin, about the same size as the mini torpedo in Z's arm, was attached to the magnet.

"What the fuck?" said Eurus.

I forced the magnet off of the skin. Eurus looked at me, confused. He handed me his knife. "Get it out of me," he said.

I cut into Eurus's arm and blood poured out, ruining my floor some more. Z poured kratos onto the cut I was making in Eurus's arm, numbing it as I went. I'm no surgeon, and I probably could never become one; my stomach's too weak. As the blood started running over my hand, I gagged and had to stop and look away to avoid emptying my stomach.

I had already cut his arm right where we expected the object to be, so Eurus went ahead and dug his fingers into the hole in his own arm. He pulled out a small torpedo-shaped object, just like the one in Z's arm, this one still in perfect condition. We checked my arm too, but there was nothing.

"It's a tracking device," I said. "Probably installed in all military members. We need to get the fuck out—now."

38/06/15AX

The night of the 35th, we had to bring a new crew member in. After we'd discovered that Eurus was being tracked, the first thing I did was ask him and Z if they knew anyone with a decent-size truck who they would trust with their lives, and whether they could get their hands on it ASAP.

"I might know a guy—my boy, Osiris," said Z. "But why can't we just use my truck?"

"We can't use any of our vehicles; we need someone to come in from the outside, someone they have no information on," I explained. "And we can't use our phones anymore, either, or even carry them with us; they have to stay in this room—except for Eurus's phone. I have two old radios we can use to communicate with when needed, and—"

"Wait, what do you mean, except for my phone?" Eurus interrupted.

"When we leave, we should tape your phone and tracking device under a random car. Give them a false trail."

"Word," said Eurus with a smirk.

"Actually, Z, go ahead and call Osiris. But use Eurus's phone to contact him and get him here. If they are tapping it, they will know we have a truck on the way. Then we can hide the phone and device under a different truck; this way when they track it, and potentially find it, they will think it's us."

"Do we have enough time for this?" asked Z. "They gotta know already that we're here."

"The tracking device most likely only gives coordinates, not elevation," I answered, "meaning, they may know we're in this building, but it has a hundred and fifty-five floors and a total of sixty-two hundred apartments. We have time."

As Z used Eurus's phone to call Osiris, I started packing up everything we would need into every box or container I could find. Almost everything was in the apartment, which made packing pretty easy. However, the vigor reactor and the oven were both still in my storage unit on the basement level of the building. We would have to get those last.

"All right, I had to call Osiris like five times before he answered, but he's on his way. He's gonna call back when he's here," said Z.

"What did you tell him?" I asked, since I hadn't heard the conversation while I was packing.

"Nothing, really; I just told him we needed him for a transport," Z replied. "The dude moves large quantities of drugs and illegal weapons for a living, so he doesn't ask many questions."

"Good."

It was about midnight when Eurus's phone rang. He answered it on speaker so Z could talk.

"Yo, I'm here. Where should I park?" asked Osiris.

Both Z and Eurus looked toward me for the answer.

"Park in the lot between buildings A and B, but as close as you can to building B; that's where we are. There should be some open parking spots right by the building. Back up so we can get everything from the building to the truck with the smallest chance of being seen."

"All right, I got you," Osiris replied in a dazed voice. "Send Z out first, so I know it's y'all. Then I'll get out and open the door."

Everyone grabbed some boxes, each of us carrying three apiece so we could take it all out in one trip. We took the elevator down and walked out to the box truck, with Z leading. It was pouring rain outside, which we hadn't known beforehand.

When Osiris saw Z, he exited the truck in a white rain jacket, unlocked the back door, and held it open for us as we put the boxes inside. Z got in the passenger seat and Eurus and I headed back into the building to get the items from my storage unit.

The basement was so dark that when I opened the door to the safe in my storage unit, the light from the reactor temporarily blinded us until our eyes adjusted. We searched for something we could safely hide the reactor in. Eurus found an old suitcase I'd forgotten I even had; it was perfect, except it was locked, and I had no idea of what the combination might be. Eurus banged the suitcase lock against the concrete wall until it opened.

"I guess that works," I said.

I put the reactor in and closed it up, but now it wouldn't stay shut. I spotted some duct tape and wrapped it around the suitcase, sealing it. I closed the storage unit, and we both carried the oven with the suitcase on top, safely loading them both into the truck. I spotted a similar white box truck further down the parking lot, and used the duct tape to attach

Eurus's phone with its tracking device under the unknown truck.

Eurus and I went back to Osiris's truck and got in the back, to make sure everything stayed safe and unbroken. We closed the door and found a safe place to sit down. Z had one radio with him, and I had the other.

"Yo, where we goin'?" asked Z over the radio.

"I don't know yet," I replied. "We still haven't found a warehouse to go to, have we?"

"I got a place in Simmerson I never really use," said Osiris. "It's nice and private, but you'll have to pay me some rent, along with paying me for this ride." He must have taken the radio from Z. "It's a two-day drive from here."

"Perfect. The farther away from here, the better," I replied. "Whatever you need for payment, I'll get it for you."

"All right. Normally I wouldn't even start something like this without some money up front, but Z is my boy and he trusts y'all, so let's go."

"Buckle up," said Z. "Ha ha—just playin'. There's no seat belts back there."

Eurus and I held onto a bar in the back to keep us from getting injured going around corners. Eurus pulled a blunt out of his shirt pocket and lit up.

"This will help the time go by faster," he said, coughing and passing it to me.

Chapter Four
GANGSTA'S PARADISE

Later, 38/06/15AX

We arrived at the hideout this morning. (I'm recording these events after the fact, as writing in the back of the box truck on the 36th and 37th was pretty much impossible; whenever I tried, I would get motion sickness.)

When we arrived in Simmerson, Osiris opened the back door for us to get out. I could actually see what he looked like now that it wasn't pouring outside. He's thin, shorter than Z and me, but taller than Eurus. He's a little older than Z, and has cornrows and a small beard.

I was happy to see that the warehouse is big enough to build the spaceship in. Although there's no door for me to get the spaceship out, since it's not a hangar, I'll just have to cross that bridge when I come to it. The best part is, it's deep in the Simmerson rain forest, where it would be almost impossible for anyone to find us.

Eurus, Z, and I started unloading the truck. Osiris looked at us, pretty confused, and said, "Those obviously ain't drugs. Don't look like no weapons I've ever seen either. What are y'all up to, anyway?"

I realized Osiris still had no idea what we were doing—just that we needed a large hideout and had a bunch of supplies. I decided we should tell him. But at the same time, if we tell him, he might not even believe us. I mean, it does sound ridiculous.

"We're building a spaceship and escaping Mars to go to Gaia," I said.

Osiris looked at the supplies, then at us. "Y'all for real?" he asked.

"Yeah, I know, right?" answered Z. "But it's for real."

"Y'all got room for one more?"

I wasn't sure if he was serious. So I answered with, "I mean, yeah . . . but are you sure you'd want to go? We could make it all the way to Gaia safely, but we could also blow up in the middle of outer space."

"Yeah, it's cool," answered Osiris. "I'm wanted in every region of Mars by the Martian Army and every region of the ocean by the Martian Navy. My brother got me into this game when I was younger; it was all I knew, ya know? But as I got older, I realized there ain't no future in this. I have no choice but to keep doing it at this point, however, because if I turned myself in, I would get the death penalty. So, an escape sounds like a pretty dope plan to me."

"All right," I replied. "Although you have to realize that we have no idea what's even on Gaia; it could be full of flesh-eating monsters for all we know."

"Don't matter," said Osiris, shaking his head. "The one thing I do know about Gaia is that no one there knows anything about my ass. So I'll take my chances against the flesh-eating monsters."

"Okay, then, you're in," I said, deciding on the spot. "As long as you can help us."

"Cool! What can I do?"

"Well, we need sheets of chazakium—a lot of them— with a width of at least a quarter centimeter," I answered.

"I'll see what I can do," Osiris said. "Anything else?"

"Well, we're gonna have to stay here till we leave in the ship. So food, clothes—the essentials."

"Cool—I'll go get those now. That's easy."

Osiris left to get the supplies I had asked for while the rest of us brought everything inside the warehouse.

It looked even bigger on the inside. It's a bit messy, but I noticed a lot of stuff we'll be able to use. There's an old welder (although I'm not yet sure it works). There's a large workbench complete with a range of basic tools. There are four stoves which were probably used for making mania (an extremely addictive and harmful drug people inject into their bloodstream), but we can clean one up and cook our food on it. And there's even a small room off to the side with six cots, more than enough for the four of us. If the welder works, I will have everything I need for the vigor converter.

It's time to start building it.

39/06/15AX

Osiris came back to the hideout late last night with food and clothes. Pretty nice clothes, too; I was surprised. All designer shit. I'm guessing he didn't pay for them—probably just lifted them from another warehouse.

"I'm picking up some sheets of chazakium tomorrow morning," said Osiris. "I called a place, and I'm gonna get there as soon as they open," he said. "I'll need some money. Shit's expensive."

I still had a decent amount of cash left from Hades. I was keeping it all in a shoe box under my cot. I gave Osiris more than enough for the chazakium, and he left this morning to get it. He should be back anytime now.

With Z and Eurus working as my assistants, the vigor converter is almost done. We don't really know how much time we have; this all needs to be done as quickly and efficiently as possible.

For the next few days I'm not gonna write much, if anything at all. I need to put all my time into this ship right now.

Osiris just got back. Gotta go help carry the stuff in.

44/06/15AX

The shell of the ship is done. When the vigor converter is activated, it essentially starts the ship. The top piece of the shell spins one way while the bottom piece spins the other, on an axis. I placed the blueprint on the next page.

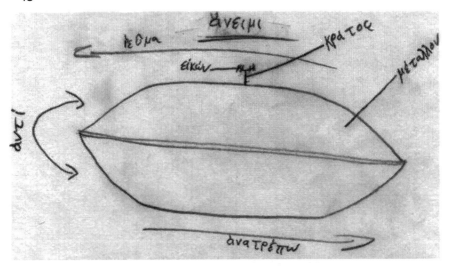

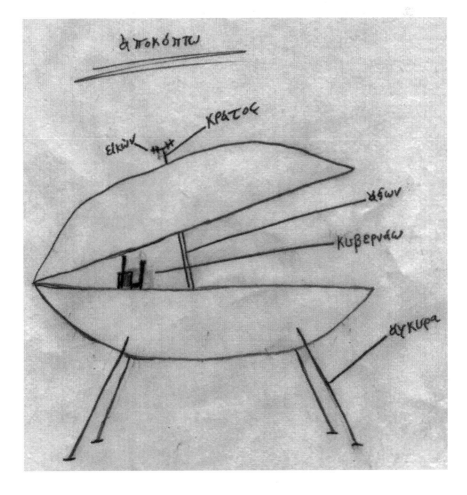

As we worked, I realized we need a lot more things to complete the ship, but Osiris is always good about getting ahold of whatever I need in a timely manner.

Although the shell is done, the rest of the ship is not. It looks pretty damn close, but more will have to be done before I can trust taking it through the atmosphere and into outer space. I've been so deeply focused on this, it keeps me awake at night. I have to smoke some asclepius every night or I'd never sleep. While I don't really mind the not sleeping, Eurus made a good point: "You're building a fuckin' spaceship, man. You can't afford to make any mistakes. You need to sleep."

The newest dilemma has been figuring out how we're gonna get this thing out of the warehouse. We knew we'd have to cut the walls or the roof, as there's no way this would fit through any existing door in the warehouse. Being a homemade spaceship, I didn't think a hole in the wall would be a good idea; it might be too hard to steer the ship out safely. The roof was a much better idea, but we had to figure out how to safely cut a hole up there. I left the decision up to Osiris, since it's his warehouse.

"I *got* this shit, y'all," he said. "I'll go up on the roof with a plasma cutter and cut out a hole large enough for us to get out, but leave some pieces attached so the aluminum roof doesn't actually fall apart. When we're ready to leave, the ship will bust right through the pre-cut aluminum, no problem."

It seemed like a pretty good plan, so he went ahead and did that.

As far as the ship itself goes, I need to add some insulation, make sure everything is airtight, and finish up the wiring for the controls. I also need to build a pressurizer, which will even out the pressure for us in space so our heads don't explode.

46/06/15AX

I've only slept a total of about six hours since the night of the 43rd. I've been working on the ship nonstop. Osiris still gets whatever I ask for, and Z and Eurus work as my assistants. While Z takes a lot of breaks, Eurus is more helpful.

"My fingers feel weird, man," Z complained the other day.

"We'd be done by now if you didn't keep taking breaks," said Eurus.

"I have carpal tunnel!" he whined.

This warehouse is pretty cool, actually—nicer than my apartment. At least there's always plenty of hot water. We could probably stay here forever if we really wanted to, but fuck that; we're going to Gaia.

Today I'm finishing up some airlock tests to ensure that the ship is safe. I am also installing the oxygen separator, which connects to an oxygen tank, filling it with oxygen from the outside and filtering out any gas that is not oxygen. I'm adding cameras to the top and bottom of the ship in the two small areas that don't spin—the axis of the ship—so we can see what's above or below us on a video screen.

Although this ship is basically the original design we created at MIPE, mark 1, it's a little bit different. The ones they have now are far more complex, and would be nearly impossible for me to build with scraps in a warehouse. This ship is big enough for the four of us to fit comfortably inside; we could maybe fit one or two more, but it would be pretty cramped at that point. It has a chazakium shell that spins at the speed of light.

The newer MIPE ships have a different way to convert the ship to a form of energy; I don't fully understand it. While the newer shells are split into two pieces, like this one, nothing is spinning. I didn't even know this until I saw the one Hades had stolen.

Whatever. This one just needs to get us one planet over.

Tomorrow is the first test run: an attempt to make the ship simply hover in the warehouse.

01/07/15AX

We applied the finishing touches this morning, basically just greasing all of the moving metal parts.

I was hesitant about doing the test run; we all were. One of us had to be inside the ship, and we were all afraid it might blow up or something. As the main builder, I felt like it was my responsibility to do the first test run.

As I walked toward the ship, Eurus stopped me.

"Let me do it," he said. "I'm the pilot. Plus, I helped you build it. I trust it."

"No. I can't have another friend die because of me," I responded.

"I'm not gonna get shot down like Hades did. I'm just gonna do a test run on the ship, not even leaving the warehouse. I helped you build this fuckin' thing, and I have enough confidence in it to put my life on the line. So if anything goes wrong, it's on me, not you."

So I stepped back and let him do what he wanted to do.

"Wait—someone already died?" asked Osiris.

Z told him what happened while Eurus and I got the ship ready for the test run.

The ship has four anchors, basically just metal rods that come out from the bottom part of the ship when landing. The top part of the ship lifts up with hydraulics, allowing crew members to enter.

Eurus activated the hydraulics while the rest of us watched intensely, nervous and excited about what was about to happen. He closed up the ship and we all just watched and waited.

I heard the humming from the vigor reactor making contact with the vigor converter, which was a good sign. The top piece of the ship began spinning slowly, gradually speeding up. As the top began to move almost at the speed of light, we could all feel a draft coming from the ship.

Eurus then activated the bottom piece and it began spinning in the opposite direction. It started up at a much faster speed than the top did. As soon as the bottom piece activated, it immediately broke all the anchors and the ship appeared to drop. The three of us braced ourselves in a panic, thinking the spinning ship was about to start bouncing around the inside of the warehouse.

But then we heard nothing but a humming sound. We looked up and witnessed the ship hovering there, gracefully. Both pieces must have hit light speed before the ship had a chance to make impact with the ground.

We all watched in awe as Eurus made the ship go up and down, then slowly hover around the inside of the warehouse. We were all smiling, happy to see the ship working.

Suddenly I heard a loud bang; as both the top and bottom pieces of the ship made a sudden stop, the ship dropped to the ground. It didn't appear to be damaged at all, which is as it should be. The shell shouldn't be affected by that short of a fall.

The three of us stood there in shock until the hydraulic top of the ship slowly opened and we heard Eurus, still alive, exclaim, "Owww!! Fuck! What the *fuck* happened?!"

"It must be a short. It's nothing; I can fix it overnight," I said.

"It doesn't feel like nothin'! My back is fucked," he said. "That's it—you get the next test run, Adam," he joked, limping out of the ship.

We were happy to see that Eurus was okay, for the most part. But as he approached us, we were startled for a second as we noticed his hand. He was probably in shock and hadn't noticed, but his hand was fucked up, as well. It must have hit against something when the ship made its sudden stop against the concrete floor.

"*Yoooooo!*" exclaimed Z. "Look at your hand, my dude."

"Oh . . . Word?" Eurus replied, as he noticed his hand. It was bent in a place where it definitely shouldn't have been, but no bones were sticking out.

Without missing a beat, Eurus smacked his hand against his thigh to snap the bones back to where they should have been.

The three of us flinched. "What the *fuck?!*" we all yelled simultaneously.

"What?" he replied. "I had to snap it back in place, and it makes the most sense to do it now while I still don't feel anything, rather than later, when it will hurt like fuck. Now I just need to wrap it in something and hope it heals."

"I'll go get some painkillers," said Osiris. "Be right back."

"All right, sounds good," I said. "I'll get started on finding this short, and building stronger anchors."

"What do I do?" asked Z.

"I don't know. Stand guard and make sure I don't blow myself up, and help Eurus if he needs anything," I answered.

02/07/15AX

Osiris came back late last night with a sling, hand brace, and painkillers for Eurus.

I located the short in the ship's wiring inside the vigor converter, the first place I checked. That's because it's the most complex piece, and therefore, has the biggest chance of containing an error.

Z watched me work for a while, and then asked, "Hey, man, how come when the ship shorted out, everything hit a sudden stop? Why didn't the two pieces keep spinning?"

"I built it to do that, just in case of an error," I replied. "If the pieces kept spinning at that speed when it hit the ground, Eurus would have ended up with a lot worse than a broken hand."

Once I was satisfied with the repair, I felt a great sense of relief, and finally got some sleep. I awoke this morning to Osiris serving some kind of hash for breakfast, which I was surprised about. Usually we all just make our own food whenever we decide we're hungry.

"I woke up before y'all and I was bored, so I decided to make some breakfast," Osiris said. "Plus, I gotta find some way to thank you for takin me off this fuckin' planet."

"Well, the ship isn't ready yet. Still gotta do test drive number two today," I said, taking some bites of the hash.

After the delicious breakfast, I took my turn at test-driving the ship. Unlike Eurus, I have never been a pilot. But since I'd built the ship, I figured piloting it couldn't be that difficult.

This time, everything worked perfectly. The new anchors didn't snap, and I was able to raise them back into the ship successfully. I made sure to let the craft hover for an extended period of time to ensure that there were no more shorts.

"So can we leave now?" Z asked as I exited the ship.

"No, not quite." I replied. "I don't want any of us to die in this thing. I wanna make it hover overnight, so we're sure it can withstand running for that much time. I'll just sleep in it. If all goes well, we leave tomorrow night."

Chapter Five
FUCK THA POLICE

03/07/15AX

I woke up this morning, proud of myself, and quite relieved to find that the ship was still running. I'm not planning a return trip, and after landing, the ship will be Eurus's problem. I personally don't know if the ship will still be in flying condition after all this. I only built it to make it to Gaia, and I know it won't last forever. I think Eurus knows that, too.

Our plan was to leave tonight. This morning, Eurus and I were the only two awake. Z and Osiris were still passed out in their beds. We decided to go on the roof with the plasma cutter and make sure there were enough cuts there for us to break out safely.

Once we were satisfied with the cuts, I said, "Watch this." I put the plasma cutter against the metal to activate it, and used the arc to light a blunt. Eurus and I just chilled on the roof, smoking, looking at the planet we would soon be leaving.

As we sat there, just bullshitting about life, we started to hear something in the distance. As it grew closer, I recognized the all-too-familiar sound. It was a Martian helifighter, again. Along the dirt road in the distance, we saw about six army trucks heading our way. Eurus and I jumped up, ran to the edge of the warehouse roof, and climbed down the ladder as quickly as we could. I jumped off once I was about halfway down, which resulted in me rolling my ankle.

"Wake up! We gotta get the fuck out of here!" Eurus yelled as we ran into the warehouse.

Z and Osiris did not respond right away, so Eurus and I ran over to the cots and shook them both awake.

"Yo—calm down! What the fuck's goin' on?" asked Z.

"They found us!" I exclaimed, "No fuckin' idea how, but they did. We gotta get on the ship now! It's the only way we can escape."

Still half asleep, Osiris asked, "Whaaa—? What are y'all freakin' out about?"

By now, the helifighter had reached the warehouse and begun using its loudspeaker.

"Adam Jelani, Ricardo Eurus, Jack Zelus, and Osiris Pookie—you are under arrest by the Martian Army. Surrender to us now or you will be executed on sight."

"Your last name is Pookie?" asked Eurus.

"Fuck you!" Osiris yelled while he and Z jumped out of their cots. We all ran to the ship, which I had already remotely opened.

"Is this shit really gonna work?" asked Z.

"Yes . . . maybe . . . I don't know! But we don't really have any other choice," I answered. "It's death, life in prison, or this. So let's go."

"Wait, we gotta name it first," said Eurus. "It's bad luck if you don't name it."

"Do we really have time for this?" I asked.

"Hades—let's just name it Hades," suggested Z.

"Word," said Eurus. "Write it on there with a marker or something and let's get the fuck out of here."

We all boarded, Z last after writing HADES with a black permanent marker along the edge of the top piece of the ship. As the ship was closing up, we witnessed men breaking down the warehouse doors. As soon as they were in, they began shooting at us, but all shots ricocheted off the ship. The top was closed before any shots could hit us.

Eurus turned on the sonar screen, so we could see what was going on. Three men had jumped on the ship and were attempting to pry it open. However, as the rotors began to spin, the men were forced off.

Once the rotors hit light speed, Eurus navigated us out of the pre-cut hole in the roof. On the sonar, we saw a missile coming toward us. Eurus tried to activate vigor speed before the missile hit, but he was too late. As the missile crashed into our ship, we were all scared for our lives, thinking this was it.

The ship kept working—it was just really warm inside. We saw another missile headed toward us on the screen, but thankfully vigor speed was activated before the missile hit, and we took off into outer space, traveling at the speed of light.

??/??/??

This is basically just an extension of my last entry. Since we've left Mars, I feel like the dates must be changed from now on. We're not on Mars anymore, so why conform to King Xavier's calendar?

Another reason the calendar must be changed is to simply make everything less confusing. A full day on Gaia is about forty-one minutes less than it is on Mars, and a Martian year is 687 days, whereas a Gaian year is 365 days.

I left the date blank for now, since we're in space, where there are no dates. I will figure out a new system once we land on Gaia, which we're about to do. Traveling at the speed of light, it only takes about fourteen minutes to get to Gaia's atmosphere from Mars, based on its current position in or orbit. We will be there in about two minutes, according to Eurus.

We will then slow down to ensure we enter the atmosphere safely, without crashing into the ground. I'll write more once we're safely at our destination.

Chapter Six
READY FOR WHATEVER

Day 1

The landing was pretty scary. But I'm writing, so obviously you know we succeeded.

The GPS unit's screen allowed us to see where we were on the planet, and ensure that we didn't land in the Gaian Ocean. It looked like we were over a small sea, with a large piece of land sticking out into it.

"Should we land there?" asked Z.

"Nah," answered Eurus. "We're still really high up in the air and moving too fast to land."

We passed over more of the small sea, then were again over land and drawing much closer. Eurus finally stopped the ship, hovering above the land. He used the video screen to make sure nothing too big, like a tree, was in the way. He got us to a nice flat area and navigated the ship close to the ground, then hit the button for the anchors. Unfortunately, there was another short and the rotors came to a sudden stop, making a loud, obnoxious noise as the ship hit the ground. At least we were okay. The ship seemed all right, other than the short. I'm guessing it was connected to the landing-gear button. Should be an easy fix.

We opened the ship and walked out. The first thing we noticed was how much warmer it was, which makes sense, being closer to the sun. I fixed the short and got the anchors out properly so the ship wasn't sitting directly on the ground. We all walked around the area for a minute or two, looking at the large pine trees and ferns. Then, Z turned to me and said, "So . . . what the *fuck* do we do now?"

"I don't know yet. Give me a second—I'm thinking," I replied.

The navigation system built into the ship had conformed its coordinate pane to the size of Gaia. Since Mars is a much smaller planet, it needed to adjust in order to accurately tell us our coordinates. The spot where we landed on Gaia was located at 38° 58' 51" N, 22° 20' 24" E. We saw no animals anywhere, but that didn't mean there weren't any. The loud bang from the ship probably scared away anything in the vicinity.

"Let's build a shelter for now," I said, "over the ship. We might need a safe place to come back to."

We each had a pistol tucked in our pants for protection if some animal ran up on us. However, we've realized that we have no clue as to what's here; maybe a pistol won't be enough. That's why I figured a shelter was the best thing to do first.

We have witnessed some life, but only plant life like trees and shrubs. We'd already assumed these were here, so it wasn't much of a discovery. These trees are much bigger than any on Mars, so I guess that's something.

The shelter is done, we made it out of some fallen tree branches and plant leaves. We're gonna get some sleep now. When we wake up, hopefully I'll be able to figure out what the fuck we do now.

Day 2

I woke up to a gunshot, which scared the hell out of me.

"What the fuck?!" Eurus and I both yelled while jumping awake.

Osiris looked like he was scared shitless, and Z was pointing to the other side of the ship.

I walked over there and jumped when I saw an enormous, feline-like animal lying dead on the ground.

"It just ran up on us. I didn't know what else to do," said Z.

"I woulda done the same thing," I said. "But now we know there are animals here—animals that could kill us. If there's one of these, there's gotta be more."

"Yeah," said Z, "but we each have a gun and plenty of ammo packed. We should be good."

"Yeah, well, I think we should look for some *intelligent* life—and a real shelter, better than what we were able to build here," I said. "We need to explore." I said.

We each had a bag filled with food, water, asclepius, extra clothes, a sleeping bag, and some other shit. I closed up the ship so no animals would be able to get in while we were gone.

"Which direction should we go?" asked Osiris.

"Let's go east," Eurus suggested. "We came in from the west and passed over a lot of land after we crossed that sea. On the radar, there was more of the sea to the east, and it's much closer than the part we flew over."

"All right, east it is," I said. "Where there is water, there may be people. I packed a compass in each backpack, and mine appears to be working on this planet, so we should be good."

I asked Eurus approximately how far from the water he thought we were, based on what the radar said. He guessed about fifty-six kilometers, so we estimated this journey would take us about twelve hours.

After a few hours, we realized our initial estimation of twelve hours was probably incorrect. The terrain is very hilly, and we're always slowing down and watching our backs. We have no idea what other animals could be watching us.

We walked east for a good fourteen hours, only stopping briefly for snack and bathroom breaks.

"This sucks, man," said Z. "We've been walking for *so* long."

"I think I actually agree with him," Eurus replied.

"What do you mean, you *actually* agree with me?" Z asked in an offended manner. "What the fuck is *that* supposed to mean?"

"Whatever—shut up," Eurus replied. "Adam, should we camp soon?"

"Not yet," I said.

Finally, we came to a clearing with a small pond. It seemed like a safe water source, since some animals similar to Martian deer were drinking out of it until they saw us and ran away. But we should also distill the water over a fire to be safe.

"This looks like a good place to set up camp," I said.

Osiris made us something to eat from what I had packed, and then we all got some sleep, rotating to have one person on lookout while the other three slept. I'm writing this while I finish my shift.

Day 3

Once we all got our sleep, we continued east after refilling our canteens with distilled water..

"So, what's the plan if we get to this sea and we still don't find any intelligent life?" asked Z.

"We walk along the coastline until we do," I answered.

"And if we never do?" asked Eurus.

"Then . . . I don't know, man."

"Why y'all ask so many questions?" said Osiris. "Just go with the flow, bro."

After four more hours of walking, we left the forest and came out on a small beach, facing the sea. Other than those deer and the occasional new bird or bug species, we hadn't really seen anything interesting.

We examined the water—very salty, similar to the Martian ocean. However, Mars has one big ocean, while Gaia has several. And this isn't an ocean, it's a sea. I could see some creatures in the water. They almost looked like some kind of insects; they had pincers, and walked sideways on the ground beneath the water.

We decided to take a small break and just chill on the Gaian beach, listening to the birds and watching the waves crash.

"Maybe we're the only intelligent life on this planet," said Z.

"Maybe, but I doubt it," I replied.

"That would be dope."

"No it wouldn't," said Eurus.

"Why not?" asked Z. "We could just chill here forever."

"Because," Osiris replied, "we didn't bring any women."

"Exactly," said Eurus.

"Oh, well, I'm bisexual," said Z.

"Wait, *really*?" I asked.

"Yeah. You got a *problem*?"

"No, it's cool," I replied. "I just did not expect that. I'm straight, though."

"Me, too," said Eurus and Osiris simultaneously.

We kept talking for a while, just about random shit. Until suddenly—

BANG!

The sound was faint, coming from the south.

"That was a gunshot," I said.

"Sounded like a pistol," said Eurus.

We all became as quiet as possible and listened very carefully, hoping to hear it again to have a better chance of identifying what it was.

We heard the sound three more times; although relatively soft, we were almost positive they were gunshots.

"All right," I said. "I guess we're heading south."

We walked south for a few more hours, but were still very tired from the distance we'd already hiked the day before. We decided to make camp, and continue heading south tomorrow.

Day 4

"I'm still tired," said Z as we all woke up. "Can't we just take a sleep day?"

"We could just leave you behind," said Eurus.

"Nah," Z replied. "I'm just playin'. I'm gettin' up."

We walked south for about eight hours, along the coastline. We didn't hear another gunshot for quite a while. We hoped if we just kept walking in that direction, we'd find something eventually.

Finally, during the eighth hour—

BANG!

We heard another shot, much louder this time.

"*Damn*," exclaimed Z. "That sounded close."

"Yeah, so be quiet," said Eurus.

We began walking toward where we thought the shot had come from, which was back in the woods and away from the sea. After a few minutes, we heard what sounded like something running in the forest. Thinking it was another cat, we all reached for our pistols and had them in our hands, ready.

It wasn't a cat, however; it was a girl, running out of the forest. As soon as she saw the four of us with guns in our hands, she began screaming violently at the top of her lungs, then fell to her knees, crying.

Chapter Seven
WE AIN'T THEM

Day 4 Continued

I signaled everyone to lower their guns as I slowly walked over to the girl. She seemed just a little younger than me.

"Shhhh . . . what's wrong?" I said softly. "Don't worry . . . we aren't gonna hurt you."

The girl's crying became fainter. She looked up at me, confused.

I realized she was definitely not Martian. Her eyes were dark brown, which was almost scary at first, as everyone on Mars has blue eyes. Her skin was a little lighter than ours—still brown, just a lighter shade than I'd seen on any Martian. Her dark hair was long, in beautiful dreadlocks. Well, the hair on her head anyway. Unlike most Martian girls, her arms and legs were pretty hairy as well. Also, she was only covered on the bottom. Her breasts were exposed, with a small amount of chest hair between them.

She looked at us like she thought we were going to kill her.

The more I spoke to her, the more it seemed she had no idea what I was saying. At first, no matter what I said, she looked like she was afraid for her life. Then, she just looked confused. I tried to think fast, to show her we were not her enemies, without using language. I sat down with my legs crossed, then placed my gun on the ground beside me. The other three guys realized what I was trying to do and did the same. I locked eyes with her and smiled.

She seemed to understand we were not going to harm her, but still looked bewildered.

Then, she spoke. "Malum."

"Ummm . . . Malum?" I responded.

She looked angry and pointed at me, yelling, "Malum!" Then, pointing at herself, "No malum!"

"My name is Adam, actually," I said. "What's your name? Nomalum?"

"Name," she said flatly.

"Yes. What is your name?" I asked with a smile.

"Eve," she said, still speaking in a quick, flat tone.

"Hello, Eve," I said, smiling. I guess she was able to understand a few Martian words after all, but not many. Perhaps there were some Martians on this planet already?

Once she had finally calmed down, we were able to get a closer look at her. She appeared to have injuries around her wrists, as though she had been struggling against handcuffs or some type of restraint.

"Hurt?" I asked, keeping my speech as simple as possible, in hopes she'd understand.

She stared at me. She no longer looked scared or confused—more content than anything else.

"Follow," she said.

I didn't know whether this meant the same thing in her language, until she started walking back in the direction she'd come from. We all got up, grabbed our guns, and followed.

I started to notice prints on the ground, from boots or shoes—Martian ones. I could see what looked like an end to the forest coming up ahead. As we approached, Eve started walking more slowly and quietly. We did the same.

I could hear someone yelling "Faster!" over and over again as we exited the forest.

What we saw next was astonishing, and very disturbing. It looked like about three hundred Gaian natives, like Eve, chopping down trees and loading Martian spaceships with them. Armed Martian soldiers were walking around, watching the Gaians and assaulting them with whips.

As I looked further to the left of the clearing, I could see soldiers throwing deceased Gaians in huge holes; they had been beaten to death. It made me sick to my stomach—even sicker when I looked at Eve and saw that she was crying again.

"Follow," I said to her.

I wasn't sure where we were at this point, so I just started walking away from the crazy tree-harvesting death camp.

I knew we had to do something about this. One of the reasons we'd wanted to go to Gaia in the first place was to escape the tyranny of the Martian Army.

"Well," said Osiris. "That was the most fucked-up thing I've ever seen in my life."

"Yeah, we need to do something," said Eurus. "We could save some of them once we learn more about when the guards make their rounds and shit."

"That sounds like a lot of work," said Z.

"It will be," I said, "but we're gonna have to do it. For now, I think we should make camp. It's getting dark." I looked at Eve. "Camp?" I asked. She looked confused again, so I assumed she didn't know that word. "Sleep," I said. Still no response. So I lay down and pretended to sleep, then looked back up at her and pointed at myself before going back to pretend sleep.

"Ah!" she exclaimed. "Yes!"

Once we'd unrolled our sleeping bags, we realized Eve had already gone to sleep on the ground, in the same way I had pretended.

Day 5

I woke up first. As I sat up and looked at my surroundings, something seemed out of place. My eyes were still blurry from sleep, so I thought I was looking at a pile of blankets or something, in the middle of where we were all sleeping.

As my eyes focused, I jumped when I realized the pile of blankets was actually one of those giant cats, just sleeping right next to us. Z was to my left, so I shook him awake and pointed out the cat, after first urging him to be quiet. Like me, he jumped as soon as he realized what it was. He reached for his gun.

"No, stop," I whispered. "It could have already killed us, but it didn't. Wait for it to wake up; don't shoot unless it looks like it will attack."

Z threw a rock at it to wake it up, which I thought was a pretty dumb idea. However, the cat just lifted its head and looked at us, then groaned as it put its head back down and closed its eyes. Confused, I threw a rock at it too, hitting it in the side. Its head shot back up as it stared at me.

"Heeyyyyy . . . good kitty," I said nervously.

The cat slowly started to stand up, stretch, and walk toward me. My heart was pounding. The animal was a little over a meter tall and over two meters long. It was mostly gray, but had some black stripes on its tail, legs, and face. As it slowly got closer to me, I noticed its bright blue eyes.

Osiris woke up at that moment, saw the cat, and immediately grabbed his gun and aimed. Before he could shoot, Eve came out of nowhere and tackled him. The gun went off, but no one was hit.

The shot woke up Eurus. We all looked at the cat, whose hair was sticking up as it stared at Osiris.

Eve hurried over to the cat and began petting it to calm it down, whispering to it in a language I didn't understand. The cat soon sat down and seemed calm again.

"You treat her good, she treat you good!" yelled Eve, while looking at Osiris, the longest sentence I'd heard her speak yet—in Martian, anyway.

I guess as long as we have Eve with us, we don't really have to be worried about getting attacked by giant alien cats anymore. And apparently this one was a female.

It was time for us to figure out what to do next. Eve is safe with us, at least for the time being. But there are still three hundred or so other Gaians at the tree-harvesting camp, let alone potentially thousands more we haven't seen yet. Eve knows how to speak some Martian, so maybe there are other Gaians who can speak even more of it than she does.

I knew we needed to figure out how to safely get more Gaians on our side, and we needed Eve's help to do it. I had to communicate with her somehow, without knowing how much Martian she actually understands.

"Do you have family?" I asked her as she continued petting the cat.

"Family," she said. Slowly, she continued "Mother . . . father . . . brother."

"Okay. What are their names?"

"Names . . . Zayn, Anubis, Ares."

She spoke faster when she was speaking their names, probably because she understood what she was saying.

"Okay, so your mother's name is Zayn, your father is Anubis, and your brother is Ares?" I confirmed.

"Yes. My family."

"They are back at that camp?" I asked.

"Ares."

"And your parents?"

"Dead."

"Oh. I'm sorry. Can we save Ares?"

"Save?" she said, looking confused.

I guess she'd never learned that word. "Can we go and get Ares?" I rephrased.

"We must," she said, smiling for the first time.

It seemed the more she spoke with me, the more comfortable and fluent her speech became. With her first smile, I realized how beautiful she really is. I felt like I'd established a real connection with her, and not like I was talking to a brick wall.

We had to get back to the slave camp where hundreds of Gaians were working against their will, and somehow rescue Eve's brother—and possibly others—without getting ourselves killed. We had guns, but so did the Martian soldiers. We would have to find a way to use stealth. It would be our only chance.

"Do you know where Ares is in the camp? Could you point him out to us?" I asked Eve.

"Yes," she said, starting to cry. "I no want to leave him. Told me to go if have chance. I did."

"Don't worry, Eve. We will get him back," I assured her.

"Why help?" she asked, looking up at me.

I didn't know what to say.

Eurus said, "Because the way our people are treating you and your planet is wrong."

"So we're gonna fuck 'em up," said a determined Z.

"You'll die," she said.

"That's not very optimistic," said Osiris.

"We need to start a revolution," I explained. "If we do that, it won't matter if we die. The revolution will be immortal."

"Revolution?" she asked.

"Yeah, probably too big of a word there, my dude," said Z.

"We must resist—fight back," I said.

Eve smiled and said, "Fight back."

"If you just get close enough to point Ares out to us, we will take it from there, considering we blend in as Martians," I said.

The others nodded, and we made preparations to go, adding silencers to our pistols. Just in case we had to take a shot, we didn't want to alert other soldiers unnecessarily.

Once we began walking back toward the camp, the cat got up and followed us. I guess we have a pet now.

By the time we got there, I realized we still didn't have much of a plan.

"So, umm, where is he?" I asked Eve.

"Uhhh . . . ," she replied.

"Hey!" we heard, coming from our left. A lone Martian solider jogged toward us.

"That's the crazy one who escaped!" he exclaimed. "You guys found her!"

TFT!

Z shot a silenced bullet in the soldier's head, and he dropped at our feet.

"*Oh!* Don't fuck with my *crew!*" yelled Z.

"Yo," said Eurus. "What's the point of having a silencer if you're gonna yell at the dead body after you shoot it?"

"My bad."

We heard a faint voice in the distance, saying *What was that?*

Everyone looked at Z; he shrugged his shoulders, like he really didn't give a shit that he'd fucked up.

Three more Martian soldiers appeared over a hill. I took out all three, simultaneously killing two with shots to the head with both of my silenced pistols, then quickly taking out the third. We all stayed quiet for a second, making sure no one else was coming.

Once we were sure it was clear, we put on the uniforms and dog tags of the dead soldiers, ensuring we'd blend in at the camp, and got ready to go. Eve stayed back behind the hill, by a large tree. The cat (Eve had started calling her Ella) stayed with her.

Before we left, Eve pointed to the tattoo on my wrist and said, "Ares. Ares has marking, too."

"What does it look like?" I asked. "Can you show us?" This would help us to identify her brother, without having to bring Eve with us, keeping her at a safe distance.

She drew a symbol on the ground, which looked like this:

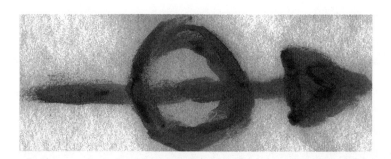

Then, she pointed to the top side of her right forearm, which I assumed was the location of the tattoo. I nodded and thanked her, reminding her to stay where she was.

We slowly made our way back up the hill that overlooked the camp.. We casually walked through the camp like it was no big deal. With about thirty Martian soldiers around, no one took a second look at us.

It was difficult for Osiris and me to keep casual expressions on our faces. Z and Eurus, as Martian soldiers themselves, are more used to acting normal in intense situations.

As we walked, I made sure to examine every arm I could see, but there were so many Gaians. As we walked further, we noticed a stairwell which seemed to mysteriously lead down into the crust of Gaia. We walked down the stairs, and when we reached the bottom, we were stopped by a Martian soldier.

"Whoa, whoa," he said. "Only soldiers with a rank of captain or higher are allowed beyond this point. You guys should know this."

This was funny, because Eurus actually *is* a captain. But, since he was wearing someone else's uniform, he couldn't just be like, "Yeah, no, I'm a captain; I just took this off a private my friend Z killed a few minutes ago." That wouldn't have gone over well.

So, we apologized and began walking away.

"What are your names? I wanna report this to your commander," the soldier said.

Since we were all facing the other direction, we were able to look at our stolen dog tags without him noticing. I was Fredrick Smith, Eurus was Scott Scottson, and Osiris was Nathaniel Levine. Z had trouble reading his. We all turned around to tell the captain our names, without any trouble, until Z spoke.

"I'm Michael . . . Paris . . . Ivy."

"Paris-ivy? But it's spelled *Para-skevi*," he said, pointing to Z's uniform, which had his fake last name printed on it. Sure enough, it said PARASKEVI, not whatever Z had said.

"Oh, yeah. Isn't that what I said?" Z responded.

"No. Let me see your ID card, Private."

"Umm, I ain't got it."

"What?! You're required to always have it with you! Who's your commander? You're coming with me," said the captain. "The rest of you are free to go."

As the three of us began walking away, the captain said, "Wait—you. Smith."

I turned around.

"You're coming too. You were leading these men into the restricted area. You're both in trouble."

I turned back around and quietly told Osiris and Eurus, "Go back to Eve and keep her safe." Then I went with the captain and Z.

We began walking toward some tents in the distance with what looked like higher-ranking officers standing around.

"What's your commander's name?" asked the captain.

We both stayed silent, not quite sure of the best way to respond.

"You guys deaf? I thought the army didn't recruit the hearing-impaired anymore," the captain said sarcastically.

Z responded before me, and I admired his attempt.

"Our commander died right in front of us, sir. We have trouble even mentioning his name without crying. We don't wanna cry, sir."

"What the fuck are you talking about?" the captain said. "There have been no Martian fatalities on Gaia in months. There's no way you've been without a commander for that long." The captain pulled out his gun and pointed it at us. "I think it's about time you guys tell me who the fuck you are."

This time, I made sure to respond before Z.

"We don't know, sir. Honest. We just woke up here with no memory of anything."

It wasn't that great of a lie, but it was all I could think of.

After a long pause, the captain responded. "Whatever. Come with me; I'm placing you two in a holding cell until this shit gets figured out."

We went peacefully, heading toward the tents and then down another stairwell similar to the last one, which led to a makeshift jail. The captain locked us in a large cell with about thirty Gaians and two other Martian soldiers, who also appeared to be prisoners and not on some sort of guard duty. When the captain left, it was just the two of us with all of these other prisoners. Once I was sure it was clear, I asked the two Martian soldiers what they were doing there. One responded, "We have souls. We tried to tell the commanders that what they do here is wrong. So now they say that makes us 'one of them,'" pointing at the Gaians.

"What are your names?" I asked.

"I'm Sergeant Christof Suelenski, and this is Sergeant Obadiah Rogers."

I looked around at the Gaians, then asked Christof, "Which one of them speaks the best Martian?"

"That would probably be me," interrupted a tall, well-built male Gaian. "I befriended a Martian a while back. They killed him for being my friend, but he taught me a lot."

He was bigger than any Gaian I'd seen, and more muscular than any Gaian *or* Martian I'd ever seen.

He walked forward to shake my hand. As our hands met, I noticed something on his arm out of the corner of my eye.

"Name's Ares," he said.

Chapter Eight
BLOOD ON THE LEAVES

Day 5 Continued

"*Ares?*" I confirmed.

"Yes. You seem surprised."

"Ares, as in Eve's brother?" I said.

"You know my sister?"

"She's waiting for us right now," said Z. "We came here to find you."

"So she's okay?"

Ares was very relieved to learn his sister was safe. Then he was all business.

"So what's the plan?" he said. "How do we get out of here?"

"Well, I mean . . . I wasn't really planning on needing to break out of a jail cell," I responded. "But I'll think of something."

We took a break and got some sleep. Well, tried too. I stayed up a bit and tried to figure out how we were going to break out of a Martian-built jail cell.

Day 6

We were woken on the morning of the sixth day by the guards opening the cell door and throwing in three more prisoners.

Z yelled to the guards, "*Hey!* Where's our phone call?!"

The guards ignored him and walked away. Once I was sure they'd gone, I spoke to Ares.

"How many other Gaians here speak Martian?"

"Fluently? None. A few probably know some words, but they're all the negative ones the Martian soldiers yell at them. They don't know how to have a real conversation."

"Well, can you communicate with them for us?" I asked.

"Of course; why?"

"We have to get everyone to work together and break out of here, then fight back against the Martians," I said, trying to sound more confident than I felt.

"Is something like that even possible? They are so much stronger than us," Ares said.

"Are they?" I asked. "I'm pretty sure they just have guns. You can fight back—all of you can."

"But how?"

"Well, first we gotta get out of here. Then, we need to get everyone out of harm's way. Once we do that, we can think of a real plan."

"And how are we gonna do that?" Z asked.

"Get everyone here to fight the next time the cell door is open; they won't expect an attack. It's only two guards; we can beat them, whether they have guns or not. Once we're out of the cell, I'll scope out the area and determine our best getaway. Pretty simple," I said.

"Doesn't sound simple," Ares said.

He was right; I knew this could go horribly wrong. There could be someone right outside the door that hears and alerts everyone else. But this was the only somewhat logical idea I could think of. "Well, it's this or wait here to die. So I suggest you tell your people the plan. Next time that door opens, we attack."

"Okay . . . Fine, mister bossy alien man," Ares replied.

Ares then spoke to the other Gaians in their language. Some looked scared; others looked excited. I told Ares, "There are only six women. Tell them they do not have to fight."

He spoke to them again, and the women looked relieved.

We all sat and waited. It took hours before the guards came down again. (I'm just assuming it was hours, as we had no clock or view of the sun.)

Finally, we heard the guards walking down the stairs. Like usual, two guards approached. They had only one prisoner with them this time, an elderly Gaian man.

One of the guards unlocked the door, and as soon as he opened it, Ares did not hesitate.

Gotta give the dude credit—he fucked that first guard up. He grabbed the cell door and slammed it right back into the guard's face, giving him an immediate bloody nose and bloody teeth. The guard fell backwards onto the ground as the second guard pulled out his pistol.

Z had already made his way up there, however, and tackled the second guard to the ground, pinning him down and punching him in the face several times. I made my way up the stairs to check out our surroundings and the possibility of a safe escape.

It looked like it would be clear as long as we waited for the perfect moment.

I went back downstairs and retrieved my and Z's pistols, and also gave the fallen guards' weapons to the other two Martians who were in the cell with us. I took one more look outside, and once I felt it was the best time, we walked out from the cells, all Martians acting as soldiers and all Gaians acting as prisoners. We casually walked back toward our campsite, where I assumed the others would be waiting.

Surprisingly, we arrived there safely. Well, kind of.

On the way, we came across a soldier returning from the edge of the woods, zipping his pants up like he had just finished urinating.

"Hey . . . umm . . . where are you taking those prisoners?" he asked.

So I shot him. I'm pretty sick of people getting in our way at this point, wasting our time.

Anyway, once we'd arrived at our little base, the others were there waiting for us.

Ares and Eve were so happy to see each other again.

"Ares here speaks very fluent Martian," I said. "He will be helping us out. He can speak to both Martians and Gaians. Because of him, we may actually be able to lead a successful rebellion."

"Sooo . . . what do we do next?" asked Osiris.

"Well, first we need a better base than this," I answered. "This place is way too open for all of us to remain hidden. We need a place to hide an army. Because an army is what we are going to build."

"And we're supposed to just free all of those Gaian prisoners from that camp?" asked Z.

Obadiah and Christof looked at each other, then back at Z.

"That camp is nothing," said Christof.

"Unfortunately, he's right," said Ares. "You really want to save all the Gaians, you will have to go to the Capital. Freeing the prisoners here at Camp 25 will be helpful, but it will not mean victory. There are forty camps in all, with about one to two hundred slaves in each. The Capital controls them all. You want victory, you'll need to attack it. It's where the Martians first land when they arrive here from Mars."

"And it's just called the Capital?" asked Eurus.

"No. They call it Atlantis," said Obadiah.

"Okay. How do we get there?" I asked.

"We go south until we hit the sea," Ares replied. "Then we need a boat of some kind. The current should take us right there."

Day 7

It is the morning of Day 7 now, and I'm ready to start heading south. I got bored waiting for everyone to get ready, so I attempted to draw Ella, the giant cat.

When we woke up this morning, Obadiah and Christof were both missing. We looked around and waited as long as we could, but we had to get moving. So, we began walking south, continuing to act our parts as Martian soldiers and Gaian prisoners, just in case we were spotted by anyone.

We walked for what seemed like forever. Ella was with us, but not right next to us. She was keeping her distance for some reason, which was fine with me. If we are spotted by anyone, it might seem kinda weird to have this monster cat with us.

"Why can't we just go back to the ship and use that to go south?" asked Z.

"It would draw too much attention, obviously," said Eurus.

"Yeah," I replied. "And the ship is too small for all of us."

"We're probably almost there," said Osiris.

As the sun went down, we still had not reached the sea. We decided to keep walking in the dark. The other Martians on the planet were most likely sleeping, and we had Ella in the distance, keeping us safe from predators.

After another hour or so, we heard a faint growling, so I put my hand up to motion everyone to stop. We stood there quietly, listening. The growling gradually became less faint as we saw the glow of eyes approaching us. At first, it was just one pair of eyes, then it was several, all around us. As they got even closer, we were able to see the animals the eyes were attached to. They were like some kind of wild dogs, all identical and in a pack.

"Eve!" yelled Z. "Can you calm these things down the same way you did with Ella?"

One of the wild dogs jumped at Z, and I shot it in midair, its dead body crashing into Z and knocking him down. This caused all the other dogs to come running for me, so Eurus, Osiris, and I shot them all.

Eve and some of the other Gaians started crying, so I felt like kind of a dick. But I didn't know what else to do—that first one was about to kill Z.

"They thought you were going to hurt us," said Ares. "They went after you to protect us."

Well, now I felt like even more of a dick.

"Ares, can you calm them down next time?" I asked.

"Well, there isn't much we could have done," Ares replied. "When they are in a pack like that, they are harder to tame. You would have had to kill them anyway, or they would have killed you and your team."

I guess that made me feel a little better, but I still hated to see Eve crying.

I went over and gave her a hug—the first time I had made physical contact with her. I wasn't sure if she even knew what a hug was, but she hugged back. I made sure to approach her cautiously; I didn't want her to think I was going to hurt her. Once we'd embraced, she slowly calmed down. I felt a strange spark between us, like the feeling you get when you kiss your crush for the first time. I didn't think I had a crush on her; I didn't even know her. We could barely communicate with each other.

As the hug ended and I backed away, I couldn't help but notice her beautiful dark dreadlocks and her unusual, haunting dark eyes.

Day 9

We got to Atlantis today. I didn't write at all yesterday because I've been so focused on just getting here. Seeing it for the first time was a strange combination of amazing and terrifying.

We walked over a hill and looked down to see the gigantic sea. Along the shore, there were several fields of crops and what looked like clam- or fish-harvesting camps. Somewhat close to shore was a small floating city perched on top of a weird, metal, barge-like thing, with buildings similar to the ones back home. In the center was a structure similar to King Xavier's castle on Mars. It would've been beautiful if it weren't for the thousands of Gaian slaves being forced to work the fields along the shore.

There was no way for us to get out to the island unless we swam through the sea. We had no idea what type of creatures might live in that water, so swimming across seemed like a terrible idea.

"All right, let's do this," said Eurus.

Osiris, Eurus, and I walked to an area along the shore that was away from the camps and fields, with Z watching from the hill just in case anything went wrong.

We saw a boat close enough to see us, so I tried to flag it down.

"Okay, everyone, just be cool," I said.

The boat started heading in our direction. They didn't seem to suspect anything until they hit shore. Once they were close enough, I said, "Hey—so we were wondering if we could hitch a ride back to th—"

"*It's him!!*" one of the four Martians on the boat yelled.

They all drew their guns and pointed them at us while one of them said, "You are under arrest by order of the Martian Army. Get in the boat. A lot of people are looking for you, Mr. Jelani."

I thought we were dead, until all four Martians were shot to death.

"*Oh!* Don't *fuck* with us!" I heard Z shout from the hill. He yelled loud enough for the Martians from the camps to hear him. They began to pursue Z and the Gaians as they ran away.

"I guess we've got a boat now," said Osiris.

The boat started to sink from the holes Z had shot into it.

"Nah," said Eurus.

"Doesn't matter," I said, looking at six more boats in a triangle formation heading our way.

Chapter Nine
NOTORIOUS THUGS

Day 9 Continued

"Well, what the fuck," said Eurus.

All six boats were now facing us, bobbing in the water close to shore.

"Take one step and we will open fire on you," said one of the Martians through a loudspeaker.

Osiris sighed before saying, "I guess it's over."

"Sorry . . . ," I said.

The Martians who'd been pursuing Z and the Gaians had caught them, and were now marching them toward us.

"No one got away?" I asked Z.

"Only Ella," he replied.

The Martians on the boats had boarded dinghies and motored to shore, and were now face-to-face with our group.

"So. If it isn't the *notorious* Adam, Zelus, and Eurus," one of them said. "And someone else . . . Who are you?"

"Ask yo momma," replied Osiris, before he was backhanded.

"The king is very excited to see you all. He's waiting back at the castle," said the man.

We boarded the boats and made our way to the city on the island. Once we'd set foot on Atlantis, the guards patted us down and threw everything into the ocean: our guns, compasses, food and water—everything except my notebook, which I'd hidden in my crotch while we were still on the boat.

The island looked amazing. Everything was still under construction, all the work being done by Gaians: processing factories for the crops they harvest for food; manufacturing plants for building new spacecrafts and vehicles; apartment buildings that still looked empty. They were trying to build an entire Martian civilization on this floating island.

King Xavier was waiting for us in his castle, at the center of the island. We couldn't talk to each other at all on the way there; Z kept trying, but was told to shut up immediately. We were all escorted through the castle until we were finally standing in front of the king.

"Most impressive—you managed to steal one of our ships," said King Xavier. "I wouldn't be so mad if you hadn't already crashed one into my son's baseball field."

"Actually, we built our own," said Eurus. "Well, Adam did most of it, but we all contributed."

"Ha ha ha ha . . . okay, sure. None of you are that smart."

"Okay," replied Eurus.

"You cost us a lot of money, destroying that ship," said the king. He looked around at all of us, then pointed at Eurus,

Osiris, and me. "To the dungeons, you three, until I figure out what to do with you. And you, Zelus—you just murdered four of my soldiers."

"Yeah—my bad," Z replied.

"You are to be chained outside in the sun, and executed tomorrow at 1200."

We all gasped, except for Z. He was probably in shock or something. Or still trying to act tough.

"And all the Gaians with you, to the fields across the waters."

I'm in the dungeons now, with Eurus and Osiris, trying to document all of this the best I can. We have to save Z, but we also have to save Eve and Ares.

First Z, because he doesn't have much time left.

Problem is, we have no idea how to do it. I need to stop writing and start working on a plan with the guys. The next time I write, hopefully we will have Z back.

Day 10

In the very early morning of the tenth day, we were trying to figure out a plan to escape and rescue Z, which seemed impossible. There was always a guard keeping watch over us, in shifts. Osiris suggested that we figure out a way to incapacitate the guard at the beginning of his shift, so we'd still have plenty of time before the next guy showed up. However, we could only whisper, and not for long, because we didn't want to draw any attention to our group. This made it even harder to formulate a plan.

Finally, out of nowhere, Eurus just got up and started talking to the guard on duty.

"What's up, man? I'm Eurus."

"I know," he replied.

"And you are?"

"Sergeant Koalemos."

Eurus extended his arm through the bars of the cell to shake the guard's hand. "Sergeant Koalemos, nice to meet—"

BANG!

Eurus had pulled him forward by the arm as hard as he could, hitting the unsuspecting Koalemos's head against the cell bars. Sadly, he wasn't knocked out.

"*Oooouuuuch!*" he exclaimed.

I didn't notice at first, because it all happened so fast, but Eurus had also grabbed the guard's gun off his belt when he'd pulled him against the cell, and now he was pointing it at him.

The guard was lying on the ground by the cell. He'd just started to reach for his radio when he noticed that his gun wasn't there anymore. He looked up to see it pointing right at him.

"Whoa, whoa—let's not do anything crazy," he said.

"Give us the radio and the key," said Eurus.

He threw us the radio and Eurus lowered the gun.

"I can't give you the key, though, because—"

Eurus raised the gun.

"—because there isn't one! *Calm down!* It's a number pad. Just let me type in the combo and everything will be cool."

The guard opened the door, and Eurus told him to get into the cell.

"C'mon, man, I opened the door," the guard replied.

"So? Get in," Eurus repeated.

The guard walked into the cell as we all walked out of it.

Osiris closed the cell door and made sure it was locked while he looked at the guard, laughing.

Eurus tossed me the gun and I led the three of us out, not entirely sure where we were going.

It was still dark. I'd been expecting to walk out and find no one around because everyone would be asleep, but I was wrong. The Gaians were working in shifts, too, many of them still hard at work, constructing the man-made island.

We had to find Z first, as he was due to be killed soon, and we didn't have much darkness left. We didn't have a clue where he might be, so we just wandered around slowly and quietly for about a half-hour. By this point, we realized we weren't making any progress.

"I say we go back to the guard we locked up and force him to tell us where Z is," suggested Osiris.

It was starting to get lighter out. It looked like the sun was going to rise in about fifteen or twenty minutes.

"I guess that's our only option right now," I replied. "I think we came from that—ow!" A rock had hit me in the leg. We all tried to figure out where it had come from, and saw what looked like Z, flipping us off with both hands. He was about forty meters away, chained in the middle of the only field I'd seen since we'd arrived on the island. Just a simple, small grass field on the other side of the road.

We quietly started walking toward him, keeping an eye out for any guards, finally running across the road to Z.

"My bad—I was aiming for Eurus," Z said as we approached him.

"Fuck you," Eurus replied.

Z had a chain locked around his ankle, about three meters long and spiked into the ground.

"Soooo, any ideas on how to get you out of this?" I asked.

"Nope," he replied. "Unless you got a key. Otherwise I'd already be out."

"Does it have a number pad?" asked Osiris sarcastically.

"What? No." Z replied.

"I guess we're gonna have to dig the spike out of the ground," I said. "That's the only thing I can think of."

"Hey!"

We heard a voice in the distance, and looked over to see a guard looking at us from the road. I thought as quickly as I could and just started shooting the ground where the spike was over and over again. More and more guards heard this and came running in our direction as clouds of dust floated up into the air from the bullet-riddled ground.

"Cover your eyes!" I yelled.

"Say that *before* you start shooting next time!" yelled Eurus.

The guards were closing in on us as Z yelled, "Duck!" He ripped the spike out from the hole I'd made and started swinging it around the top of his head as fast as he could. The guards didn't see it because of the dust, and ran right into a spike flying around in their faces.

Eurus grabbed a gun off a fallen guard and tossed it to Osiris, then grabbed another one, and the four of us ran off in a random direction for cover. Eurus, Osiris, and I were shooting at the guards coming toward us as Z continued hitting them with his spike-and-chain weapon when they got too close. Eventually Z caught up to us and we started making our way toward the sea, until we heard shooting again; then we would get back to cover and shoot back.

Finally the sea was in sight, and we ran toward it as fast as we could. When we were about fifteen meters away, the enemy gunfire started again, so we all got back under cover.

All except Osiris.

"*Osiris!!* Get behind something!" yelled Z.

"I got this!" Osiris shouted back, still running. "I'm gettin' the fuck off this piece-of-shit isl—"

BANG BANG BANG!

Three shots hit his back, and he fell into the sea he'd been about to jump into.

He was gone.

None of us reacted for about five seconds, just looked back in shock.

Then, I saw Z start to stand up, mouth wide open, yelling "*AHHHHHHHH!! YOU MOTHERFUCKING MOTHER FUCKERRRRRRRRRS!!*"

I knew he was the only one without a gun, and I thought we were about to lose him, after all we'd done to try and rescue him.

I got up and started shooting every enemy I could see before they could shoot Z. Eurus started doing the same. Everyone was so focused on the two of us that they didn't even see or hear Z running up on them with his spike-and-chain affair. He started tearing the guards apart, whipping the chain and spike at everyone he saw. Dead guards were falling everywhere, from either gunshots or chain hits, until there was not a single one left; they were either dead, or they'd run away.

I threw my pistol to the ground and grabbed two better-looking ones off some dead bodies and put them in the back of my pants. I also grabbed a couple of extra mags, pretty long ones, too.

Eurus threw his gun and grabbed an assault rifle. I didn't really see what Z grabbed, but I did see him stuffing some weapons into his pants as well.

We hopped into one of the boats and took off back toward shore, to find Eve and Ares. That's where we're at now—making camp, and working on a plan to find them safely.

I'll write more later, we need to finally get some sleep. While we talked, I made this drawing of Atlantis:

*   *   *

Even though she doesn't know much Martian and she looks a lot different than the women I'm used to, I woke up missing Eve quite a bit. I seem to be having . . . like, romantic feelings toward her. It's weird. Is it weird? I don't know.

I had a dream that we both lived back on Mars together. We were in a nice house in the middle of nowhere, two kids and a dog. Osiris was in the dream; he came to visit. That's when I woke up. It kinda ruined the dream and made me feel depressed.

"Do we have a funeral?" asked Eurus. "Like when Hades died."

"Hell yeah, we're doin' a funeral," Z replied.

We all said a few words. I ended with, "Osiris is with Hades now. As terrible as this is, hopefully this will at least remind us that we have to finish this. Like Eurus said when Hades died—Osiris's death can't be meaningless."

"Why didn't he just get under cover?" asked Z. "He'd still be here."

"I don't know," I replied. "But we have to keep moving. Do you know which way they took Eve and Ares?"

"Toward the shore," Z replied. "The same way we went. I didn't see where they went after that."

We decided to check the closest farming area, the one we'd passed on our way here. We obviously couldn't just walk in. We got as close as we could, then Z climbed up a tree.

"What do you see?" I asked.

"Leaves, man," Z replied. "And branches. Some bugs."

"I mean, at the farm."

"Nah, man, I can't see shit over there. Too many leaves."

"Go up higher," suggested Eurus.

Z pulled a joint out of his bag and lit it up.

"Go *up* higher," said Eurus, "not *get* higher."

"Oh, my bad," Z replied.

He started climbing up higher, eventually getting to a spot where he could see through the leaves.

"All right, I see a bunch of Gaians, farming and getting whipped and shit."

"Yeah, we know that. But do you see Eve or Ares?" I asked.

He learned forward and used one of his hands to shade his eyes, trying to get a better look.

"Yeah! Yeah, I see Ares!"

"What about Eve?"

"Umm . . . oh shit," said Z. He'd dropped his joint, and started trying to reach down to pick it up.

"What the hell are you doing?" I asked.

"I dropped my shit. One second."

CRACK!

The branch snapped and Z fell all the way down, hitting about four other branches on his way down. He hit the ground and the spike on his chain stuck into the ground right next to his head. He was okay—just bruised and scratched up a bit. He'd had the wind knocked out of him, so he was overreacting like he was paralyzed.

"Just go without me! Leave me to die! Finish the mission," he exclaimed—right before Eurus grabbed his hand and pulled him to his feet.

"Don't be a baby. Let's go," said Eurus.

"Did you see Eve?" I asked again.

"Damn, anybody even gonna ask if I'm okay?"

"You okay?" I asked.

"No, my knee hurts."

"Okay, so did you see Eve?"

"No, man. I mean, I don't think so. But I don't know for sure. I know I saw Ares, though. That beefy motherfucka can't be missed."

"Well, that's good enough for me," said Eurus. "Let's go."

"Let's wait until it's dark," I suggested. "We got off that weird island in the dark, so we can do the same when we rescue Ares and Eve."

"And another one of us can die?" said Z. "You expect me to get killed just because you got a crush on that alien?"

"You just told us to leave you to die, like, two minutes ago," said Eurus.

"Yeah, plus you've already followed us this far. Do you have anything better to do?" I asked. "And we're not only saving Eve and Ares. We're just . . . saving them first. We could use their help. We're gonna save as many of these Gaians as we can."

"So it's just the three of us versus the entire Martian Army?" asked Z.

"The three of us and the Gaians," I replied. "We can call them the Gaian Army."

"Adam," Z said, putting his palm to his face, "they've only got, like, rocks and sharp sticks and shit."

"Yeah, I'm working on that."

I wasn't, though. Not yet. I was hoping Ares could help with figuring out how to arm our forces, since he seems pretty good at speaking Martian. We could probably make some bows and arrows for them or something. I don't know.

But I did know we'd have to wait until nightfall to go in. So in the meantime, we just sat around, smoked some joints, and told some stories about Osiris to help ease the pain. We hadn't known him very long—well, at least, Eurus and I hadn't—but he still died for us. Making him more loyal than some people I've known my whole life.

Finally, it was starting to get dark. We still had the guard's radio; if they spotted us, we'd most likely hear about it over that.

"I'll wait out here and be a lookout," said Z.

"A lookout for what?" asked Eurus. "There are already guards in there."

"I don't know. For more of them, I guess."

"You're just scared," said Eurus with a laugh.

"Fuck you guys. My knee still hurts. It's probably infected or something, but you guys don't even give a shit."

"I'll grab you something to put on it while we're in there," I said.

"Thank you, *Adam*," Z responded sarcastically.

So the plan was simple: I gave Eurus the radio. I was going to walk in, casually, acting like a normal Martian soldier heading toward the area where all the Gaian slaves sleep. If I got all the way to Ares and got him out without being seen, great. Mission successful. If not, or if Eurus heard anything over the radio about me or saw someone coming toward me, he would run toward me, acting like another soldier, tackling me and acting like he was taking me back to Atlantis.

I also had my two pistols in the back of my pants, if needed. Eurus had his rifle.

Z was by the exit where we would run out, if necessary, with his spike-and-chain weapon set up as a tripwire.

"Can anyone explain to me why Adam has two guns and all I have is a damn chain locked to my ankle? The fuck am I supposed to do with this?"

"Because you want to wait out here," Eurus replied.

"No, before that. I already didn't have a gun, and he's had two since we left that crazy floating island."

"I thought I saw you putting a gun in your pants or something when we were leaving the island?" I said.

"Nah," Z replied.

"Fine; I'll grab you a gun if I see one. Anything else you need while we're in there?"

"Some cheesy puffs, if you see any; I've been craving them so bad. Like, *for real.*"

I started walking in. I could see the area where all the Gaians were sleeping, so I casually walked in that direction. I had part of my face covered, so hopefully they wouldn't recognize me. I was walking along the perimeter instead of just heading straight toward the Gaians.

I saw some medical supplies, some of which might help with Z's knee, but didn't grab anything yet. I decided to wait and grab them on the way out.

As I approached the Gaians, the ones who were still awake shook in fear as I walked by. I could see Ares. He was awake, but not looking at me. As I walked up next to him, he said, "Oh, am I to be tortured again? You shouldn't have come alone. I can overpower you, tiny Martian."

I showed my face. "It's me. I'm here to break you and your sister out."

He turned and looked at me, still not showing much emotion at all. "Well, then, we better get going, huh?"

"Yeah. Where's Eve?" I asked.

"You mean, you don't know? How are you going to break her out if you do not know where she is?"

"I figured she was with you," I replied.

"I wish. Come on—let's go before they find you."

I started walking back the way I'd come.

"No, this way," he said. "I come and go a lot. I know how to sneak in and out."

"Why not just stay out?" I asked.

"My people need me."

"Sooo . . . why not break them all out?"

"Don't be so impatient, little one. The revolution is coming. And it must be fought from the inside."

"So, why are you leaving with me now, then?" I asked.

"So many questions from a species who thinks they know everything."

"Okay, well I don't have time for riddles, or whatever this is," I replied. "Let's just get out of here and find Eve."

"Yet you do not know where she is."

"You do," I said.

"How can you be so sure?"

"Because you're leaving with me."

Couldn't get the image of Eve out of my head; thought it might help if I tried to draw her.

Chapter Ten
LOADED BASES

Day 11

Ares brought us to one of his hideouts last night, and then told us where Eve is.

It's really stupid. She's still on Atlantis. Apparently, right after we left and King Xavier ordered the Gaians to the fields, he said, "No, wait. That female right there can stay."

I don't understand why; maybe because he just wanted to separate her from Ares.

We've gotten on and off that island before, but they will be more prepared for us next time. I only wish we'd known before that she was still on Atlantis. I can't believe we left her there.

This morning, I had to ask Ares, "So, this revolution you mentioned. What's the plan?"

"We must destroy Atlantis," he replied.

"Great, so . . . like, how?"

"I was hoping you would figure that part out, Martian. Your people built it."

"Even if we do destroy Atlantis," said Eurus, "they have more ships with more people back on Mars, and they'll just come right back down here and kill everyone."

"They will kill all of us eventually if we do nothing," Ares replied.

"Do you have an army?" I asked.

"Yes."

"So what are we gonna arm them with?" asked Z. "Sharpened sticks?"

"No," Ares replied. "*These*." He moved a hidden rock door, revealing . . . a lot of spears.

"Yeah, that's what I said," said Z.

"What? No," Ares replied, "these aren't sharp sticks. I've improved the design. These are sticks with sharp, jagged rocks at the tip."

Z looked like he couldn't even think of something to say, which was a first. So he just shook his head and looked at me. Eurus was laughing.

"We're gonna need something else," I said. "Ares, how big is your army?"

"Right now, about five hundred. Could get that number up to about eight hundred if we can find more camps."

"Damn," said Eurus.

"Where they all hidin' at?" asked Z.

"Everywhere. Each camp averages about a hundred Gaians at one time. They can have up to two hundred and fifty when they first capture new Gaians, but they soon die off, and the Martians don't try to find new Gaians until they're down to about eighty or so. The bigger camps have an average of two hundred Gaians, and Atlantis has about the same. I've gone in and out of five camps myself, in addition to Atlantis."

"Oh shit, you survived that hell, too?" asked Z.

"Well, unlike you, they never knew I was there," Ares explained. "I was only there to figure out how to destroy the place. But it's so massive; I still don't know how to go about it."

"We sink it," said Eurus.

"What?" I asked.

"It's floating. We just need to figure out how it's floating, then make it not float anymore."

"We would have to get the two hundred Gaians off first. Especially Eve," I said.

"What is it with you and this cave chick, Adam?" asked Z.

"What? She's Ares's sister, so obviously saving her is a priority," I replied.

"Nahhhhh . . . you just want some of that indigenous booty."

"I don't understand that term," said Ares.

"That's probably a good thing," said Eurus.

"I don't know what you're talking about," I said.

"It's okay, I respect it," replied Z.

"Anyway," I said, changing the subject, "we can't steal five to eight hundred guns. We will have to arm your soldiers with something else, other than sticks."

"Bow and arrow?" suggested Eurus.

"Oh, Eurus got *all* the ideas today," said Z.

It wasn't a bad idea. I have some experience hunting back home with a bow and arrow.

"What is a bow?" asked Ares.

"It's a device that shoots sharp sticks," said Z. "Small ones, though—not the ones you got."

"We would have to train all the Gaians how to use it," I explained. "Which will be hard, considering they're all inside camps. Ares, why did you say the revolution has to happen from the inside? Why can't we form an army on the outside and go in to save the others?"

"They would kill them all before we got a chance to save them," he replied.

"Sooo . . . we sneak them out all at once," I said. "From every camp we know of. There's four of us. Ares, you bring us to all the camps you know and show us how to get in and out. We could do it all in one night."

"They would start looking for us as soon as they noticed," said Ares. "We wouldn't have much time. And they would kill every Gaian they could find while looking for us."

"There is no way to do this where Gaians don't die," I said. "They're dying *right now*—and like you said, if we do nothing, we all die anyway."

We came to the conclusion that our main goal tonight would be finding a safe place where we could bring the Gaians after freeing them. Ares showed us a place, which is where we are right now. It's a cave. The biggest one I've ever seen. The location is 37° 56′ 47″ N, 23° 49′ 42″ E.

Tomorrow will be the next step. He will show us how to get in and out of the camps. And most of all, in and out of Atlantis. Last time we were there, the three of us almost died. And one of us did. RIP Osiris. I'll make sure you didn't die for nothing.

We also need some kind of door or something to cover the entrance to the cave, or they will probably find us. But I don't know right now, I'm very tired.

There is charcoal here from someone who was here before us. Looks like they were using it for drawing, as the walls have pictures of animals, and Gaians, and us. The Martians. Killing them.

Day 12
We couldn't start going into the camps to practice with Ares until late, so in the morning, Eurus and I made bows and arrows. The bows were made out of wood with a hide string, and the arrows were made from sticks with stone tips and feathers.

"I see you still do not have a gun," Ares said to Z. "Perhaps I could show you the way of the spear?"

"I guess it's better than this fuckin' chain attached to my ankle," Z replied.

At this point, Z seemed pretty used to having the chain, keeping it casually hanging over his left shoulder when he isn't using it. He doesn't even trip over it. But I knew he still wanted it off.

"Let me see the chain," I said. "We should probably get it off before Atlantis, anyway. Just in case you need to swim."

Using a couple of sticks, I started trying to pick the lock, but the sticks kept breaking.

"I already tried this, like, a thousand times," said Z. "The sticks always break."

I removed the magazine from one of my pistols and took out the spring that was inside. I straightened it to use it to pick the lock, ruining the mag. Luckily I have an extra one for each gun.

"Well, I woulda tried that if I had a gun," said Z.

After about another minute or so, the lock opened. Z's ankle looked pretty bad, all cut up from the cuff on the chain. But at least now it was finally off.

"*Damnnn*," Z exclaimed. "I feel so much lighter now. I'm free, mothafuckas!!" he yelled, running around in circles.

Ares took Z spear-hunting, right after he showed us two stolen radios he had.

We decided to keep ours to listen to the guards when they're close, and then I rewired his two to work only with each other, on a different frequency, so we can communicate with each other.

Eurus and I took a short break from making the bows to look around the cave, to figure out how we will do everything.

"Where are all of the Gaians gonna fit?" asked Eurus. "There's enough room for them, but not enough room to shoot arrows without killing each other."

"Well, we have the radio," I said, "so the cave could just be the hiding spot. We could work with a small amount of Gaians at a time, outside, where they can shoot arrows. The majority of them will stay in the cave and we will switch out shifts."

"All right, word."

Ares had already been using this cave as a hideout for a while, so there was plenty of food stored up, at least for now. We will need a lot more when there are five hundred of us. It's good that he's teaching Z how to spear-hunt right now, as it's obviously a lot quieter than hunting with a gun, especially since we no longer have any silencers.

By the time it started getting dark, Eurus and I had made two hundred bows and about a thousand arrows. We would still need at least two hundred more bows and four thousand arrows, total, allotting one hundred arrows to each bow. At least we'd made a good dent.

"My hands are all fucked up now," said Eurus.

"Yeah, mine too," I replied.

Finally, when Ares and Z returned, it was dark enough for us to go with Ares to practice getting in and out of the camps.

"It's about damn time," said Z. "Let's do this shit."

The regular camps seemed pretty easy; they're all set up basically the same way as the one where we found Ares. All of the Gaians sleep in the same area, and are guarded by four guards. The guards will have to be taken out by bow and arrow, one at a time, without the others noticing. Then we'll wake up all the Gaians and have them follow us out.

The only one of us who speaks Gaian is Ares, so he will have to teach us a few basic phrases, like "Follow me" and "I'm here to save you"—stuff like that. Once we have them all in one place, Ares can translate for us.

When we felt confident we could hit the camps, no problem, we went to Atlantis. I knew it was going to be tough, because Eve was there. We wouldn't be able to break her out yet; we can't break her out until we break everyone out.

When we got to the shore, Ares immediately began walking into the water.

"Wait," I said, "we're just gonna swim across?"

"Well, yes," Ares replied. "Come on."

Z ran into the water and dove under. Guess he's still excited to have that chain off.

Eurus and I walked in slowly.

"I guess this works," I said, "as long as all the Gaians we save can swim."

"They can," Ares replied.

We just kept swimming until we were close enough to reach the ladders that extended down from the land. As we climbed up, I tried to get a good look at how the island floats. It is shaped in the same way as a boat or a barge, made of steel. If we caused enough damage, we could probably create a hole and sink it.

The sleeping area on Atlantis differed from those at any of the camps. Here they were keeping the Gaians in horse stalls, with eight guards—two at the entrance, two at the back door, and four walking up and down the stalls. They weren't guarding the windows very well, however, which is how we were able to look in and make our observations.

It looked like they were no longer making the Gaians work constantly in shifts, probably because the city was nearing completion.

I didn't see Eve anywhere.

"Do you see her?" I asked Ares.

"No. I didn't see her last time, either; I was hoping she was just blocked by someone else in front of her."

"Maybe she is this time, too," I replied.

"No," he said. "This is the eighth time I've checked. I've looked every night."

"But you said she was here," said Z.

"She is. Or was. Unless—"

"Unless what?" I asked.

"Unless she didn't last."

"Meaning?" asked Eurus.

"She might be at the bottom of the sea with all of the others who didn't make it."

I realized he was telling us she might be dead, and I felt a rage building up inside me. Ares seemed upset too, but also like he was handling it better than I was. He was probably used to it, which is really sad. Hopefully, Eve is still in there. I can't let myself believe she is gone.

We are back at the cave now, building more bows and arrows with our blistered hands. Z and Ares are helping now. It took Ares a few tries before he got it right, but I'm happy with all the help we can get.

"Am I gonna have to use one of these?" asked Z. "I still don't have a gun."

"I'll make you a crossbow," I said.

"For real?"

"Yeah, after all of these bows are done."

Z started working faster.

We should be done with the bows tonight, and close to done with the arrows.

Day 13

We finished the five hundred bows and more than enough arrows last night. And I even made a kinda crappy wooden crossbow for Z to use. I also gave him a backup regular bow if that one breaks. Ares insisted on using his spears, and had six on his back. We kept the bows and arrows in the cave, except for the ones we'll be using to take out the guards.

We went to the camps just like we planned, then all met back at the cave with the Gaians. Overall I counted about 483 Gaians, give or take. Some of them still looked scared, but most of them looked relieved to finally be out of those camps. Many of them were coming up to us, thanking us in Gaian, which sounded something like *Grotieza tebe*. I don't know; it was something like that.

Now it was time for us to hit Atlantis. The hardest camp to get to, and the one with the most guards. Plus, it's not even really a camp; it's more of a base.

Unfortunately, I can't say this went exactly as planned. I had my dual pistols, but the plan was to use only the bows, for stealth. Eurus also had his assault rifle, just in case.

"This is a really long walk," said Z.

"We're nearly there," Ares said.

"You said that, like, a while ago, though."

"You're making this worse," said Eurus. "We just did this walk yesterday."

"Yeah, but it feels longer now," Z replied. "And I have this heavy fuckin' crossbow."

"Crossbows are pretty cool, though," I said.

"Yeah, I guess," Z replied as he admired the crossbow in his hands.

We got to the shore, looking across the sea to Atlantis. I'm pretty sure we said a few words to each other, but I don't really remember.

Z strapped his crossbow to his back and we swam across to the same part of the island we'd gone to the last time. We made our way to the horse stalls, remaining undetected. The first four guards to worry about were the ones at the doors. There were two at each door, so the four of us all shot at the same time.

So far, so good. Now there were four more on the inside which we took out through the windows. All the guards surrounding the stalls were now dead.

We stormed in and Ares immediately began translating for me. I asked the Gaians if Eve was there, and when they responded, Ares began crying. I thought she must be dead. I was in shock, but trying to finish the mission. I started to get the Gaians moving, but Ares wouldn't budge.

"We have to go—she's gone," I said, my eyes tearing up. "We will avenge her."

"She's not gone," he said, angrily.

I thought maybe he was in denial or something, until he said, "Your king has her."

"Wait, what?" I asked.

"He has her as his personal prisoner," Ares said. He tried to explain further, but he was too upset.

As I thought of all the horrible things King Xavier could be forcing her to do, it felt like I was starting to black out. I didn't, because I still remember it; however, it felt like I wasn't in control anymore; anger was.

I looked at the castle in the center of the city and just started walking toward it, taking out every guard I saw with an arrow before they could see me. I had forty arrows in total. Eurus tried to stop me, but I told him to go back with the others and get the Gaians into the cave. I was going to get Eve.

"This is crazy," said Eurus. "Do you really think you can make it all the way to King Xavier? You don't even know where he is."

"I know he's in there somewhere. I'll find him."

"Nah, I'm going with you."

At this point, I didn't care either way, so we headed off together. We successfully reached the door, which was locked—until I kicked it open. So much for being quiet, but I was pissed off. We knew where the king's throne was located, and I assumed his quarters must be nearby.

I saw the shadow of a guard who was about to walk into the area where we were hiding, behind a wall. When the guard came into sight, I went up behind him with one of my guns and put it to his head.

"Where is King Xavier?" I asked.

"In his quarters," the guard said nervously. "It's back the way I just came from."

I backed away from the guard, looked at Eurus, and gave him a nod. Right before he shot the guard with an arrow. We made our way toward the king's quarters, and sure enough, saw big double doors with designs carved into them. They were locked, so I knocked.

"Sergeant Franks? Back already?" I heard, the voice getting louder as King Xavier got closer to the door. "You shouldn't be back this quickly; we will have to take a look at that—"

BANG!

The moment he opened the door I held my gun up to his head and pulled the trigger, shooting him through the forehead before he'd even had time to react to seeing me.

Chapter Eleven
MURDER WAS THE CASE

Day 13 Continued

"What the *fuck*?!" yelled Eurus. "What happened to being *quiet?!*"

"Well, you're the one yelling," I said.

"Everyone in the castle must have heard that!"

"How about we just calm down."

"Calm down?"

"Shhhhh," I said, with my index finger over my lips.

"Calm down?" he said in a softer voice. "You just shot the king of Mars in the face with a forty-caliber pistol. We were supposed to use the bows."

"I was out of ammo," I explained.

"I would've given you an arrow if you'd just asked me."

"Oops," I said, while looking into the king's quarters.

"Whatever," Eurus replied. "Let's just get out of here."

"One second," I said. I'd just seen Eve, much skinnier than before and barely awake, lying on the floor in the corner of the room.

"Time to go," I said, as I put her over my shoulder.

We ran out of the castle this time, killing any guards we saw on the way. Eurus was doing it with his bow and arrows; I planned to join in with the gun only if it was necessary.

We made it all the way to the front door before Eurus ran out of arrows. So now we both had our guns out, killing the remaining guards we saw. We got to the stables and there was no sign of anyone. They must have already made it across the sea and back toward the cave.

I jumped into the water with Eve on my back, alongside Eurus, and we swam across to the shore, Martians shooting at us all the while. Eurus occasionally looked back and fired off some shots. I couldn't shoot because I was trying to keep Eve's head above water.

Somehow, we made it the shore alive. Now we were sprinting, Eve still on my back. As my hearing gradually came back (after losing it temporarily to the gunfire), I started to hear what sounded like helifighters in our area. We were staying under the trees as we ran, so they couldn't see us, but it was still scary hearing them, knowing they were looking for us and would shoot us on sight. The last time we'd heard them, we were escaping Mars.

After running for a while, the sounds started to fade. Finally, we could see the cave. I put Eve down to help Eurus push the stone door over. As soon as I tried to do so, I felt an incredible pain that caused me to drop to the ground. I had been shot in the arm but hadn't noticed until now. As I sat there in pain, holding my arm with my head leaning against the door, I could hear Z talking to Ares from inside.

"So, with Adam and Eurus presumed dead, I'm in charge of this operation now," said Z. "Understand?"

"Fuck you!" I whispered fiercely through the crack, not wanting anyone else to hear. "Open the door!"

Ares pulled the door off using handles on the inside.

"For future reference," I said to Z, "if we die, Ares is in charge before you are."

"Man, he ain't even a Martian," Z replied.

"He speaks better Martian, though," said Eurus.

When we got inside, I put Eve down and sat next to her as two Gaian women ran up to us to tend our wounds.

Ares was crying, in shock at seeing Eve again.

"We thought you died," said Z.

"Yeah, I realize that," I replied. "Honestly, I'm surprised we didn't."

"But wait—how did you get Eve?"

"Oh, yeah, about that. Change of plans," I said.

"He shot King Xavier in the face with a pistol at point-blank range," said Eurus.

"*What?!*" yelled Z. "Are you out of your *damn* mind?!"

"Maybe a little," I replied. "We aren't gonna have time to train five hundred Gaians how to shoot a bow and arrow. They're already after us."

"After you," said Z. "I ain't done shit."

"What?" said Eurus. "You've killed your fair share of Martians, too."

"We still have a ship, man," said Z. "We could just leave right now and go back to Mars."

"We are wanted by the Martian Army," I said. "They will kill us there too."

Out of nowhere, we heard a helifighter fly right over the cave.

"Okay, eventually they have to stop and go back to Atlantis, right?" I said. "So we just wait it out. Then—"

"No!" said Z. "Give me one reason why any of us should listen to you. You just made this whole thing a thousand times worse."

Ares picked Z up by his shirt and slammed him against the cave wall before saying, "Because he just saved my sister's life, and he was able to get in and out of that castle without getting killed. If you have a problem with it, I'll kill you before any Martian."

"My bad," said Z, laughing nervously.

"So, anyway," said Eurus, "what's the plan?"

"Let's get rid of any light in the cave," I said, "and just go to sleep and wait it out. I can't think right now. We will start fresh tomorrow."

"So for now we just sleep?" Asked Z

"Yeah."

Days 14-18

"We have to sink Atlantis—*now*," I said, while shaking Eurus awake on the morning of the fourteenth day. "Before they have the chance to find us."

"Umm, okay, but how?" Eurus said, slowly waking up. "There's no way we could shoot a hole in it; the metal is way too thick."

"What about an explosive?" I asked. "We could stick it directly to the hull, as close to the water as possible."

"Maybe if it was big enough—but where would we get one?"

"We would have to make it ourselves," I said. "Let's start taking apart as many bullets as we can spare. We'll need the gunpowder."

As we were doing that, Z came up to us and said, "What are you dudes doin'?"

"Trying to make a bomb of some kind," I replied.

"Oh, will this help?" he asked, putting a grenade right in front of me.

"What the *fuck?!*" I exclaimed. "How long have you had this?"

"I have three, since the first time we were on Atlantis. Never really felt the need to use them."

"Well, what the hell?" I said, still confused. "All right, let me have all three."

"My bad; you guys didn't tell me what you were doing," said Z.

"You didn't tell us you had three grenades," Eurus replied.

"Yeah, you right."

I knew the grenades by themselves still wouldn't be enough, but we could use the powder from them, and one of the detonators. The powder would still have to go inside of something bigger.

After I disassembled the grenades, I had Z and Eurus keep taking apart the bullets while I looked around for something we could use.

Ares asked what I was looking for. I didn't think he would understand, because I knew he wouldn't know what an explosive is, or how one works. So I just said, "I'm looking for something hollow and strong."

"Like a skull?" he asked.

"Kind of," I replied. "But it has to be something with no holes in it."

"A tusk."

"Like an elephant tusk?" I asked. "You have elephants around here?"

"Hairy ones, yes. Further north. But I have some tusks hidden nearby. We use the ivory to make spear heads."

"How big are they?"

"Taller than you. But not by much."

"Okay, well go get one. Hurry. We don't have much time."

A tusk taller than me is bigger than any tusk on Mars. I wasn't sure how much powder we would need, but I knew it was more than we had. So I went back to helping with the bullets while we waited for Ares to return.

It didn't take him long at all. Only about half of this kind of tusk is hollow, so we broke off the half we didn't need and put all the powder we had into the hollow half. After disassembling bullets for about two more hours, we finally had it filled to the top. I inserted the detonator and attached it to a long fuse I made from cloth and gunpowder, then plugged the opening to the tusk with a rock. I estimated the fuse would last about two minutes before detonation, so I'd have time to swim away.

"Okay, now what?" asked Z.

"Now we go do this," I replied.

"All of us?" asked Eurus.

"No, just the three of us. Everyone else will stay in the cave."

Some Gaians gave me a natural adhesive they had made right before we left, so I could stick the tusk to the hull.

Eve was still weak from King Xavier not giving her enough food or water, but she was slowly looking and sounding better. She has been helping some other Gaians gather fruit and veggies; it is helping her regain her strength. She prefers to sleep next to me at night now; she says it makes her feel safer. I'm not complaining. I left my journal with her, just in case anything happened to me.

We started making our way towards Atlantis. The tusk was pretty heavy, so Z and Eurus carried it together while I made sure our path was clear.

"Yo, we're gonna die," said Z, out of breath.

"Calm down," I said.

"I mean, he might be right," said Eurus.

"We'll be fine . . . probably."

It was dark by the time we got to Atlantis. We found an opening farther down the shore than usual, so there would be less chance of being noticed. I had to swim across by myself; too many people would make it more noticeable.

"You sure you wanna go by yourself?" asked Eurus.

"Yeah, it will be easy." I replied. "Be right back."

I had the tusk sealed up in a piece of hide to prevent water from ruining the fuse. Luckily, it was much lighter in the water, so carrying it wasn't too difficult.

I stuck the tusk to the hull as close to the waterline as possible. However, as soon as I ignited the fuse, two Martians appeared right above me. They couldn't see the tusk; they just thought I was trying to sneak onto the island.

They held me at gunpoint and told me to climb up; then they searched me and took my guns. This took about a minute, so there was still one minute left until detonation.

They began asking me questions—I don't really remember what. I was too busy counting down in my head. Then, the explosion happened.

BANG!

The island started to fall at a slight angle, the damaged side slowly sinking deeper into the water as people ran around, trying to figure out what to do. Buildings were falling over and crashing into other buildings.

"What the hell was that, *traitor?!*" yelled one of the Martians.

"An explosion," I replied.

"Smartass. Where?"

"Where you found me. But you can't fix it—not before this whole place is underwater."

He grabbed his radio and said, "Code Bird—I repeat, Code Bird."

"What the hell does that mean?" I asked.

"You'll see," said the other guard.

All of a sudden, water started shooting up from all sides of the island as the ground started to level back out. The mist cleared, and I was shocked to notice that we were levitating out of the water. The island wasn't floating anymore; it was flying. And it was getting higher and higher into the air, until we were just beneath the clouds.

I obviously hadn't been expecting this. I was in shock, trying to think of what to do next. I was wondering what Z and Eurus would think when they realized I was on this island that was now hundreds of feet above the sea. I was so busy thinking about all of this, I didn't realize that the Martians around me were trying to talk to me.

"*Move!*" one of them yelled, sticking the barrel of his gun into my spine.

"Uh, where?" I asked.

"Forward."

"There's nothing over there," I replied.

"Just keep moving."

I walked forward until I was standing at the very edge of the island. Somehow I was admiring the beautiful view, since that was the only good thing I could focus on in that moment.

The guard pressed his gun even harder into my spine and said, "Now jump, traitor."

Chapter Twelve
LIFE'S A BITCH

Days 14-18 Continued

I didn't have a choice. I was close enough to the edge that even if I'd refused, they could just push me over or shoot me. I was busy trying to figure out if it would be possible for me to hit the water in such a way that I could still survive. I figured my best bet would be feet first, in a pencil dive.

I closed my eyes, and right as I was about to jump, I heard, "*Wait!*"

The pressure of the gun on my spine was relieved, and I turned around. There was a man standing there. He looked important, but I had never seen him before.

"Bring him to me. I would like to have a conversation with this man," he said.

The guards escorted me over to him, and he said, "Walk with me."

"Who the hell are you?" I asked.

"I saved your life. Does it really matter?"

"Yeah, it matters," I replied. "I don't know how much longer you plan to let me live—or why you saved me in the first place."

"I am the highest-ranking military officer on this planet, making me the acting king. And you . . . You are the best damn soldier I have ever seen. You're just on the wrong side."

"I'm not a soldier. I'm a scientist."

"Well, I've never seen a scientist do half the stuff you've done. Unfortunately, you're just trying to prevent the inevitable."

"Oh yeah? And what's that?" I asked.

"Mars is running out of resources. Our home, *your* home, is running out of food, fuel and wood. It is necessary for the sake of our survival that we do what we are doing here."

"Have you ever considered reasoning with the Gaians?" I asked. "Maybe make some trades with them rather than enslaving them like a bunch of psychopaths?"

"They're just animals, Adam."

"You are the only ones acting like animals." I replied.

I wasn't used to strangers knowing my name. I never thought this would go this far. Less than a month ago, no one knew who I was. Now I'm wanted for stealing a Martian spacecraft and murdering King Xavier. I never thought my life could change so substantially in such a brief period of time. If I did, I might have done it sooner.

After a short pause, the man asked, "What would I have to do to get you to join our cause?"

"Change your cause," I replied.

"What if I told you that you didn't have a choice?"

"I'd prove you wrong. What is your name, again?" I asked.

"General Horus," he responded, "How can you possibly win against the entire Martian military? What is your plan, exactly?"

"We're gonna keep killing you all until you get off this planet forever," I said with a smile.

"Hmm . . . I don't see that working. I gotta say, Adam, I thought you would have a much better plan than that. We have way more people back on Mars ready to come fight. And we can definitely outgun you."

"Not all of them will want to fight," I said. "Some will see how crazy you are and join my side."

"Don't count on that. Even if we have to drop a nuke on all of you and move to a different location on the planet, zero enemy units survive."

"What if you piss people off there, too? And the same thing happens again."

"We have plenty of nukes."

"You really don't realize that what you're doing is wrong?" I asked in disbelief.

"Well, that's one person's opinion."

"Actually, about five hundred people would agree," I replied. "And that's just the ones who know about it."

"Those. Are. *Not*. People," Horus said, getting angry now.

"Look, man—if you're gonna kill me, can we speed this shit up?" I asked. "Get it over with."

"Why would I want to kill you, Adam? I want you to join us."

"I'd rather you just killed me."

He pointed his assault rifle at me and said, "You don't have a choice. Zero enemy units survive."

"Well, obviously I *do* have a choice," I said. "It's do what you say or get shot. I choose to get shot. So, do it."

Horus scuffed and looked away for a second, enough time for me to grab his gun with both hands and twist it away from his grasp. I pointed it back at him and shot him down.

I can't believe that worked, I thought.

Other Martians heard the shots and came running, so first I shot the guards who found me, taking back my pistols. Then I threw the rifle, took cover, and shot everyone I saw. It felt like it took forever—they just kept coming. I don't know how I lasted as long as I did. One shot grazed my right forearm, but that was it.

Eventually, I didn't see anyone anymore. I knew there still had to be Martians out there, but they were probably hiding at this point, waiting for me to come out.

I was close to the edge of Atlantis. I saw a chain that I guessed was being used as an anchor or something. I tucked one of my pistols into the back of my pants, grabbed the chain with one hand while holding the second pistol in my other hand, and jumped off the island. The chain was pretty long; I hadn't fully thought this plan through.

When I'd stopped falling and the chain had straightened out, I held on—just barely. I'd pulled my shoulder out and the chain had ripped up the palm of my hand pretty severely. I was in a lot of pain, and still closer to the island than I was to the water below.

I could see four rockets above me, attached to the bottom of Atlantis, allowing it to fly. I started shooting at one of them until I'd almost emptied the mag. Finally, it shut down; the island wasn't level anymore, but it was still flying with the three rockets. I started shooting at another rocket, emptied the mag, and switched the pistol out for my other one. I emptied that one too, but the rocket was still working.

I thought I was fucked at that point, until finally, the rocket started to flicker and shut down.

That's about as much as I remember.

*   *   *

I woke up four days later in the cave with Ares, Z, Eurus, Eve, and the Gaians. They told me that the island had fallen, crashing into the water. I must have gotten a concussion as I hit and forgot the previous minute or so. Eurus and Z had been watching the whole time, and had seen me dangling from the chain, so they'd had a pretty good idea of where to find me. They got me to shore and carried me back to camp.

I still can't believe I was even alive, and neither can they.

It's nighttime on the eighteenth day, and I have just enough energy to write.

We still have to do something soon. Atlantis may be gone, but I know this isn't over. Back to work tomorrow.

Day 19

I told everyone about the conversation I'd had with General Horus. The part everyone was most worried about was the nukes. Well, by everyone, I mean Eurus, Z, and myself. No one else knows what a nuke is. Even so, Ares brought up a pretty good idea.

"What if we nuke them first?" he asked.

Z rolled his eyes and said, "We don't have a nu—"

"Wait," I said. "That might work."

"How?" asked Eurus.

"Yeah," said Z, "like I was saying before you rudely interrupted me. We don't have a nuke."

"But *they* do," I responded. "They have a lot. And they're remotely detonated."

"So . . . you wanna detonate all their nukes?" asked Eurus. "How?"

"Well, it's too far to do from here. We would have to go back to Mars and figure out how to rig them all, then take off and detonate them while we're leaving the atmosphere."

"Just when I think you can't possibly think of anything more insane," said Z.

"Well, they have an entire planet full of people they can keep sending down here," I said. "Their nukes are scattered all across Mars. If we detonated every single one—"

"It would destroy the entire planet," said Eurus. "But there's still people there. People we don't have a fight with."

"Well, it's either we destroy that planet, or they destroy this one," I replied. "Mars has been dying for a long time, and the people there have been getting worse and worse. Gaia might actually have a chance at civilized humanity. Mars lost that chance *long* before Xavier."

"You're talking about destroying the world," said Eurus.

"Yeah. Or saving it," I said.

"So, we're just gonna live on Gaia forever?" asked Z. "Meaning I gotta date one of them cave people?"

"Unless you've got someone back on Mars you wanna bring here."

"Nah."

"Then yeah."

"All right, whatever," said Eurus. "What do we do?"

"We gotta get back to the ship," I replied.

The ship was 177 kilometers away from us now, and it would take us about four days to walk there. I gave the GPS unit to Ares and told him to get as far away as he could with the remaining Gaians he had, which numbered around four hundred.

"How do I use this?" he asked.

"Don't touch anything on it; just keep it with you," I replied. "If and when we get back, I can use the one on the ship to find you guys. But for now, in case we fail and they nuke the area, get as far away as you can."

I said good-bye to Eve. She's speaking much better Martian now, and has mostly recovered from her time on Atlantis.

"Why can't I go with you?" she asked.

"It's too dangerous," I replied.

"Seems pretty dangerous here, too," she said, with a little bit of a smile.

"Yeah," I replied, "but I think you have a better chance with your brother right now than with me. We are going to a place where they have never seen your people before."

"Well, that's dumb," she said. "Promise to come back."

"I don't want to promise you something if I'm not sure I can keep it."

She looked into my eyes as tears fell from her own. "I'll never forget you," she said, before we embraced.

Z looked at me disapprovingly as I walked back toward him and Eurus.

"How do you even know you can have kids with her?" Z asked. "They might come out fucked up."

I ignored him and started packing up everything I needed, and suggested they do the same. I was ready first, and I've been writing this entry while waiting for those two.

Day 20

It's morning on the twentieth day. I'm up early, and haven't woken the other two yet. We're completely out of asclepius now, which sucks. Hopefully we can find more back on Mars. I don't know how long we'll be there, but hopefully not too long.

I'm worried that this idea might be a little too crazy and we won't be able to pull it off, but we have to try.

The walk yesterday wasn't too bad, I guess. We all have blisters, so walking anywhere at all is painful, but after a while you don't feel the pain anymore.

We passed more camps that still have Gaians; too bad we can't save them all. When we get back, if we successfully destroy Mars, we'll just have to kill off the remaining Martians here and that should be the end of it. The only problem is, we've only seen one small area of an entire planet. I have no idea how many Martians or camps or bases there are in other areas of the planet. Obviously we can't bomb this planet too, so we will have to either hunt them all down or lure them to us.

I've been thinking about what Z said—about whether I can even have healthy kids with Eve. He might be right, but I don't know. I just know that the way I feel about her is like nothing I've ever felt before about anyone on Mars. That's probably why I'm okay with everyone there dying to save everyone here.

My parents died a long time ago, and I'm an only child. My only friend was Hades, and he died. Now I just have Z and Eurus, who I only met because of Hades. They're the only Martians I care about now. I don't know much about their families, though; maybe I'll try to bring that up on the walk today.

Yesterday while we were walking, it was a little awkward at first, because I felt like Z and Eurus were thinking I might be losing my mind. I had to bring it up.

"You guys do understand why I'm doing this, right?" I asked.

"Yeah," said Eurus.

"Unfortunately," said Z.

"But how are we going to do it?" asked Eurus.

"I don't know exactly. Is there anyone we know on Mars who could help us?" I asked.

"I have no idea what has been going on there since we left," Eurus replied, "so it's hard to say."

"Guys," said Z, "I just remembered something from back on Mars that will help. Only thing is, you never take anything I say seriously."

"That's because you never say anything serious," said Eurus.

"What is it?" I asked.

"The Martian Army was working on a new kind of nuke, one that was supposed to be stronger than any we've ever seen before," he said. "I overheard some engineers talking about it, so of course I kept listening. But after a while it seemed like they must have been talking about a video game or something, because, like, why would we need a nuke that big when Mars is a united planet? But now it makes sense. It could be meant for Gaia."

"Seriously?" said Eurus. "That's not helpful. That means they could potentially destroy all of Gaia with one bomb."

"It is helpful, *Ricardo*," said Z, "because if we blow up Mars first, these could detonate too."

"Don't call me Ricardo," said Eurus.

"What else do you know about these nukes?" I asked Z.

"Only what I said," he replied. "Maybe I can find out more when we get back to Mars."

We didn't bring much food with us. Since the Gaians have already shown us which fruits and plants can be eaten and which can't, we just grab food as we go. Makes for less weight to carry.

I've been worrying about what will happen to the Gaians if we fail. I know they will still fight, but the nukes will still be available to the Martians. So if we fail, Gaia fails. It's a pretty surreal feeling, knowing the fate of two entire planets is in my hands. I feel like none of this is real. Like any minute now, I'll wake up on Mars and realize I'm still living my normal life, and this was all a dream.

I've never really believed in God too much, nor does anyone on Mars. They used to, but there were so many different religions, most of the time it only led to people arguing over who was right. Eventually, it led to a generation of Martians who believed that if there were so many different religions, they must all be wrong. I used to say, "What if they're *all* right? Just not a hundred percent right. Maybe every single religion has some degree of truth to it, along with some lies." But people didn't like that, so I started to go along with the majority.

However, after my experience here—after the ridiculous, unexplainable shit I have survived—it sure feels like someone, someone greater than myself, wants me to finish this alive. Maybe that's just the lack of energy talking, or maybe I'm dying from being on a planet with a level of gravity I'm not used to, and my brain is slowly deteriorating. Whatever it is, I'm choosing to believe it's the truth. Because that, and Eve, are the only things still giving me motivation to do this and not just give up and die.

Z is waking up now, so we're gonna try to get Eurus up and start walking. I'll write more tomorrow night.

Day 21

The walk yesterday and today was a lot more painful. I stopped for a second to check the blisters on my feet, which I probably shouldn't have done; I should have just ignored them. The heel of my left sock was actually bloody. Some parts were dried from the day before, and the newer parts were bright red.

I saw a plant the Gaians showed me—I guess it's antibacterial. I don't have a med kit anymore, so it will have to do. It didn't make it hurt any less, but I wasn't too worried about the pain. I was more worried about an infection, since we still have a day's walk left.

Finally, I asked the question that's been on my mind.

"So, do you guys have any family or anything back on Mars?"

"Nah," said Z. "None I care about anyway."

Eurus was silent.

"And you?" I asked him.

"I don't know," he said.

"Well, you might wanna find out," I replied. "We can save them if we need to."

"I don't think I'm gonna be able to find out," he said, looking down, depressed.

"Why not?" I asked.

"I was an orphan," he replied.

"Well, what about your adoptive parents?"

"My adoptive parent is the Martian Army," he said, picking his head back up. "I was eight and still not adopted, because of the scar on my face. At that age, they force you to join the army. The army raises you."

"Wait, I'm confused," said Z. "I thought you got that scar from being in the army."

"No. I have no idea where I got it from, but my birth parents probably know."

"Any idea where they are?" I asked.

"Nope. And I don't really care."

We didn't talk too much more after that, trying to save energy.

At one point, it started to downpour. This isn't the first time it has rained since we got here, but this was the worst so far. It didn't bother us though, as it was actually pretty refreshing.

We passed a few Gaians today, and of course they were immediately scared of us. I know some Gaian from what Eve and Ares have taught me, so I told them we weren't going to hurt them. They still ran off, though. Either my Gaian is poor, or they just didn't believe me. I'm hoping when we get back, we can get some other Martians on our side. If we have more Martians fighting for the Gaians, maybe they'll stop being so afraid of us.

We should reach the ship tomorrow, if my calculations are correct. Well, where the ship was. Hopefully it's still there.

"So, what's the plan if the ship isn't there?" asked Eurus, when I brought it up. "Or if it's damaged beyond repair?"

Z started to rap, because Eurus had rhymed.

> *Yo, if the ship ain't there,*
> *or damaged beyond repair,*
> *that would be quite a scare,*
> *but who even fuckin' cares—*
> *cuz Adam will find a way*
> *to get us in the air.*
> *Ayyyeeeeee!*

"What he said," I said.

We are making camp now. Next time I write, we should be at the ship's location.

Day 22

Well, the ship *was* there, but it was surrounded by Martian soldiers. They were examining it, trying to figure out how it got there, I'm assuming. We saw them before they saw us, so we hid behind some trees.

"How many are there?" I asked.

"I count twelve," answered Eurus.

"Everyone got ammo?"

"Yeah," they both said.

"All right," I replied. "Fuck taking our time and hiding in cover like we normally do. They won't be expecting this. Let's just ambush them and kill 'em all before they have time to react! One . . . two—"

"Wait," said Z.

"For the *fuck what*?" asked Eurus.

"I have to fix my underwear. I have a wedgie. I can't shoot if I'm uncomfortable."

"*Goddammit.*"

I repeated, "One . . . two . . . three!"

We all came out from behind the trees and opened fire on the Martians around the ship. Well, Eurus and I did.

"*Shit*, my safety was on," said Z as he messed with his gun. We'd already killed everyone by the time he fixed it.

"What the fuck, Z," said Eurus.

"Let's go," I said.

"Where we going?" asked Eurus.

"Mars," said Z.

"Yeah, no shit," Eurus replied. "Where on Mars?"

"Who do you know that could help us?" I asked. "Anyone that might have access to nuclear weapons?"

"No," they said in unison.

"What about a hacker?" I asked.

"Nope," said Eurus.

"I know a guy," said Z. "Perses. Best hacker I've ever met, or heard of, even."

"Great. Where is he?" I asked.

"Should still be in Kylamont," he responded.

"Where the hell is that?"

"It's a military base," said Eurus. "But it's on the other side of the planet from where we're from. How do you know him?"

"He got caught," Z replied, "back when I was working as a police officer. And he sort of . . . well, he helped me sell drugs over the Internet. He never told them about me, which gave me crazy respect for the dude. I did everything I could to get him a deal, and finally, they said he could either go work at Kylamont, or go to prison. So, he's probably still there."

"All right, let's go," I said.

"Wait," said Eurus. "How good can he be if he got caught?"

"He's amazing," Z said. "He just fucked up once, got too comfortable. It doesn't matter; I know if anyone can actually pull this off, it's him."

"Whatever," Eurus replied. "I guess he sounds like our only choice."

The flight was a little scary, as the ship was making some weird noises. We were a little worried it might blow up, but it didn't.

We landed at 4° 13′ 14″ S, 71° 1′ 29″ E on Mars, thirty-two kilometers away from Kylamont. The anchors worked correctly this time, too. We didn't want to land too close, because it's a military base and they would see us. And, obviously, we couldn't just walk right in there either. We had to get into contact with Perses somehow and have him meet us.

We covered the ship up with a bunch of branches and leaves and dirt. Not the best camouflage, but hopefully it will be good enough.

It was really weird to be back on Mars. Everything seemed normal, more or less. There were fewer guards around, but I've never been to this part of Mars; maybe it's always like this here. Also, there wasn't the slightest indication that the people on Mars knew anything about the death of King Xavier, which was really bizarre.

"Can you call Perses or something?" I asked Z.

"With what phone?" he responded.

"I don't know—borrow one."

"You think I know his number by heart?"

"Well, where might we be able to find him?" I asked. "Other than the base."

"I don't know," Z replied. "We've talked once in a while, and we're pen pals. But he doesn't tell me every little thing he does."

"Wait—you're pen pals?" Eurus asked. "So you know his address?"

"Oh," said Z. "Yeah."

"And where's that?" I asked.

"About forty kilometers away. It's in Salalanda," said Z.

"Does he live alone?"

"Yeah—at least he did last I knew."

"Well, let's wait till later and go knocking," I suggested.

We found some asclepius from some random guy who just walked up to us and said, "Hey, you guys wanna buy some drugs?"

"I mean, yeah," I replied, "but I don't have any money."

"I do," said Z.

"How the *fuck* can you *possibly* still have money on you?" asked Eurus.

"Because I didn't have anywhere to spend it on Gaia, *obviously*," he replied.

We bought the asclepius and I asked the guy, "Have there always been so few guards around here?"

"Nope," he replied. "They keep sending them to other places. Not sure where; I guess it's classified."

I figure it's safe to assume they must be sending them to Gaia. So even after we destroy Mars, if we do that successfully, we're gonna need an even crazier plan to get rid of all the guards on Gaia. But I guess we'll cross that bridge when we get there.

We smoked a few joints, waiting for it to get dark. The guy we bought the stuff from hung around with us while we talked, his name was Heka. We were reminiscing about when we used to live normalish lives on Mars, even though Heka had no idea what we were talking about. Finally, we decided it had gotten late enough to go to Perses's house.

Heka drove while Z navigated. After he'd dropped us off, we knocked on the door of the one-story house. A man wearing glasses, a little shorter than me, with bushy hair like mine, but a little longer, answered the door.

"You Perses?" I asked.

"Who's asking?" he replied, in a high voice.

"What up?" said Z.

"*Jack!!* Dude, I thought you *died!*"

"Yeah, it's a long story. Can you let us in?"

He did. The house was a mess, but it was gonna get blown up anyway, so who am I to judge? I explained the situation to him, and he was a little skeptical.

"You . . . you want me to detonate every single nuke on Mars?"

"Yeah," I said.

"And we just fly off into the sunset, to Gaia?"

"Yeah, basically," I replied.

"Can you do it?" asked Eurus.

"I think so," said Perses. "As long as we're gone and get them detonated before the army finds out and kicks my door down. But what's in it for me?"

"Paradise on Gaia," I said. "And life. Because if you don't do this, we'll just find someone else to do it."

"Okay . . . Well, it's going to be the hardest hack I've ever done," Perses said. "I'll start planning how to do it right away; it might take a day or two to figure out. You guys are more than welcome to crash here in the meantime."

We were all pretty tired, so we let Perses start working while we each took a shower and changed into some clean clothes that Perses gave us, which felt amazing. We were also finally able to properly clean and bandage all of our wounds.

The antibacterial plants and hide bandages on Gaia are okay, but it felt great to finally have real medical supplies again.

After we were all cleaned up, we found places to sleep. I'm in my spot now, having trouble falling asleep. I just don't want to let Eve down, or Ares. Or Z and Eurus.

Chapter Thirteen
DROP THE WORLD

Day 23

We woke up to Perses burning breakfast and throwing the burnt pan into a pile of moldy dishes, where I'm assuming the sink used to be.

"Anyone want eggs?" he asked.

"Uhhhh, thanks," said Z. "I'm good. Got anything else?"

"I don't like eggs," said Eurus.

"Okay, I have some potato chips you guys can have. That's about it," replied Perses. "What about you?" he asked, looking at me.

"I mean, I'll eat the non-burnt parts. With a lot of salt," I said.

Z and Eurus looked at me like I was crazy for eating it, but whatever; it's food. While eating, I asked Perses, "Did you figure out how to nuke Mars yet?"

"Umm . . . well, kinda," he replied. "Like I said, it's going to be very difficult. But if you guys managed to find a way to get to Gaia and back, I guess I can find a way to do this.

I don't want you going to anyone else. If anyone's gonna blow up Mars by hacking nuclear launch codes, it's gonna be me."

"How can we help?" I asked.

"Don't know yet."

"How long do you think it will take?" asked Eurus. "You said a day or two yesterday. Is that still the case?"

"I should be ready by tomorrow, or the day after," Perses replied. "Or the day after that."

"Okay, well, we're wanted by the government," said Z. "We can't show our faces around too much."

"Really? I haven't heard of anything."

"They think we're on Gaia still," said Eurus. "But we gotta play it safe."

"Oh, that's cool," Perses replied. "I got video games and stuff. You guys can just do whatever; I'll let you know when I need help."

"One more thing," said Z. "There's a new kind of nuke the army was working on. Something huge. Can you find out more about it?"

Perses looked slightly concerned, and said, "Sure, but then there will be more of a chance I get caught."

"Then work faster," Z replied.

Z and I played a racecar video game that Perses had. Eurus threw out all the garbage in the house, which was a lot. There were more things in the house that were garbage than not, leaving a bad smell in the house—well, an even worse smell than before. I guess Eurus moved something that was moldy and it released the odor into the air.

I was having fun, just waiting for Perses to figure this shit out. It was nice being in a house, even a disgusting one, instead of being in the woods constantly watching our backs to stay hidden from Martian guards. Plus, it was nice to eat Martian food again, instead of alien plants and animals on Gaia (although I'm pretty sure I could get used to eating them).

Once this war is over and we're back on Gaia, we need to help the Gaians start living in a more-civilized way. Build a real town, not like Atlantis. Have a house with Eve and a kid or two. But none of that will be possible until we either wipe out all the Martians or get them on our side. Unfortunately, it will be even harder to convince them to be on our side after we blow up their planet. I'm still not sure if this is the best thing to do; I just know it's the best thing I've thought of at this point.

Perses has spent most of the day hacking into government bases, trying to reach the nuclear weapons area. He's successfully hacked four locations; however, there are a total of 162 bases, plus potential secret ones. He also needs to figure out how to detonate all the nukes at once. We can do 162 bombs, one at a time, but they could figure out how to stop it before we finish. We need one kill switch with all 162 bombs connected to it.

Perses knows this, but first, he has to figure out how to access all of them in the first place.

Day 24

Perses started making breakfast again this morning, but Z stopped him and said, "Nah, dude, I got it this time." Z made grits and bacon, which tasted pretty amazing. I started thinking about how much I love bacon, and that I might never have anything as good on Gaia. Then I remembered that I had seen some pig-like creatures. They just looked less evolved—hairy, with tusks. I bet they'll make some pretty good bacon. I'll find out when we get back.

I'm still enjoying our time here, just eating and playing games with Z and Eurus while Perses does all the complicated work. He's a nice guy; just a little weird. He's saying we should be ready by tonight. He has accessed all 162 bomb locations and hacked all the way into the launch command. We don't want them to launch too far—just explode exactly where they are. But they are programmed to launch first, so he is going to set it up so they detonate one second after launch. They should be about ten feet in the air at that point.

"Hey, Jack," said Perses. "I did find out about those new nukes, but a little late."

"What do you mean, a little late?" asked Z.

"I found them after already hacking into the other ones. These new ones would kill everyone on Mars just by themselves."

"So, they are going to detonate along with the other normal nukes?" I asked.

"Yeah," Perses replied. "There's four of them, and their explosion is a thousand times larger than a normal nuke."

"What the *fuck?*" asked Eurus. "Why?"

"I don't know," said Perses, "but four explosions like that—"

"Would destroy the entire atmosphere," I said. "The planet would never be able to host life again."

"Yeah."

"Well, who cares?" asked Z. "It wouldn't be able to host life for thousands of years anyway, with the radiation from all the normal nukes."

"Yeah," I said. "We can't have Perses hacking back in and risking getting caught. So I guess we have to hope that in the future, our species never wants to move back to Mars. So, Perses, is there anyone you want to bring with us?"

"Just my cat," he said, smiling. He started applying the finishing touches.

Z, Eurus, and I got everything packed up that we would need, including food, water, and medical supplies.

"How long do you think the timer should be set for?" Perses asked.

"What?" asked Z.

"Well, I won't be able to detonate it from the ship. It has to be detonated from this computer. So, I can set a timer and when that time runs out, it will detonate."

"Shit, I don't know if I like that idea," Z replied. "What if we get back to the ship and it ain't there? Or it doesn't work? Then we're dead as shit."

"That's a good point," Perses replied. "I could probably find a way to detonate it from my phone, but I would still need a timer, the signal most likely won't be strong enough to penetrate trough the atmosphere from space. I could start the timer right as we're taking off, and we know that everything is working."

"I guess that sounds better," said Z.

After talking for a while, we decided we would leave at midnight, tonight. There aren't too many guards around, but there will be even fewer at midnight. Plus, we will have a much better chance of getting it done without being seen. We're still armed, of course. If a fight is necessary, we should be able to handle it.

Perses started working on installing the kill switch to his phone, which took most of the day. I guess it was harder than he thought. After getting everything packed up, we just played video games, waiting for Perses to finish up.

"This will be the last time we ever get to play video games; you know that, right?" I said.

"Fuck that," Z replied. "I'm bringing this shit with us."

"There's no electricity on Gaia, you idiot," said Eurus.

"Someday there will be. And I'll be ready when there is."

"That could take decades, or centuries," I said. "We will be long gone."

"I'll figure it out," Z said.

We decided that since Z insisted on bringing the TV and gaming system, he was carrying that shit by himself. Eurus and I would handle the food, water, and med kit.

At about 2030, Perses finished up the last of what he had to do. It would be about an hour's walk to the ship, maybe an hour and a half with all the stuff we were carrying. We didn't want to ask anyone for a ride, because then we would feel obligated to bring them with us instead of letting them die. And Perses doesn't have a car, which was a shitty surprise.

We played games until about 2230. It might have been a waste of time, but even if Z does reinvent electricity someday, it will take a long time. We had to enjoy this while we still could. At 2230, I wrote this entry.

It's almost 2300 now, which is when we are planning to leave.

Hopefully the next time I write, I will be on Gaia again. And I will be with Eve. I miss her, and hate being apart. But I trust Ares to make sure they both stay alive.

It's time to go now.

Day 25

We left right after I finished my last entry.

There were no guards around; it was surprisingly dead. Eurus and I were carrying the food and water. Perses had the med kit and his fluffy black kitten, Bastet. Z, of course, was carrying the gaming system, games, and TV. The TV was big, but it was very thin and light, so it wasn't that hard for him to walk; it was harder for him to see. Whenever he tripped a little, it was impossible for Eurus and me not to laugh.

"You guys ain't gonna be laughin' when I reinvent electricity and scrape you in *Motorsport 5*," he said. He hadn't won any of the games we'd played at Perses's house, so I'm not sure what he was talking about.

When we finally got to the ship, it was exactly the way we'd left it, still covered in branches and leaves and dirt. We put the stuff we were carrying down and began cleaning off the ship.

Once that was done, Eurus got in and started it up. He got it in hover mode, which was enough proof for everyone that it still worked; then he landed it so we could get in.

"Ready to start that timer?" I said to Perses.

"Yup," he replied. "Getting it started now."

"How long is it set for?" asked Z.

"Fifteen minutes. I figured that's enough time for us to get into space."

"That's more than enough time," I replied. "All right, everybody in. Let's go."

As Z and I headed for the ship, we heard Perses say "Wait."

"No," said Z. "We're goin'."

"What's wrong?" I asked.

"It isn't working."

Z walked up to Perses, saying angrily, "What the *fuck* do you *mean*, it *ain't workin'*?!"

"I don't know. I didn't have a way to test it. I just trusted it would work, but it doesn't."

"So what the fuck do we do now, Perses?" asked Z.

"I guess . . . well, someone could detonate it manually," he said. "But they would die."

"No shit," said Z. There was a pause, followed by Z saying, "I'll do it."

"No," I said. "I'll do it."

"Goddammit, Adam—let me be the hero!" Z yelled.

"No. I got you into this. It's all my fault. I'll do it."

"You have Eve! I don't have shit, except a TV with nothing to plug it into," Z replied.

"You will find someone too," I said. "I have to do this."

"I'm not gonna let you do it," he said.

"How are you gonna stop me?"

"I'll shoot you, mothafucka," he said, reaching for his gun.

"No, I am—"

"I'll do it," Perses interrupted.

"Okay," said Z—too quickly, I thought.

"Just take Bastet," Perses said, handing me the fluffy black kitten. "Give her a new life on Gaia, too."

I didn't know what to say for a moment. "Are you sure?" I said quietly.

"Yes," Perses replied. "I'm sure."

I didn't really try to stop Perses. He was a cool dude and all, helpful, but only with computers. I didn't think he would last long on Gaia, but I didn't wanna tell him that.

Z and I packed the ship with the bags and the TV, and Perses ran off, back to his house.

"Where's Perses?" Eurus asked as we boarded the ship.

"Being the hero," said Z.

I explained what had happened.

"And we're taking his cat with us?"

"Yeah, I guess," I said.

"Damn." Eurus said while looking distraught, "We will have to tell people about him, he can't be forgotten."

"Yeah. He might be a little strange, but he is the most courageous man I've ever met. He might be the biggest hero of us all."

"Whatever." Z said, agitated. "How do we know he's even gonna do it? He could be runnin' off to turn us in for some reward."

"Well, you were the one who trusted him before any of us." I reminded Z. "But either way, we have to leave now. We will stop outside of Mars' atmosphere and watch to see if he actually does it."

"Fine."

After checking the ship's systems and taking another look at our navigation instruments, we took off. When we were far away from Mars, but still close enough to see it, we stopped.

We sat there silently, watching Mars from the video screen in the ship, until finally, it happened. We didn't hear it, or really see any explosion, because we were too far away. Out of nowhere, the entire planet just turned to smoke—nothing but a big gray sphere in the distance.

I think it's safe to say that it worked.

Part of me felt like saving the ship after we'd returned to Gaia, so I could come back after the smoke had settled to see what it looked like. At this point I'm sure everyone on Mars is dead. Although I did feel bad, I couldn't show it; I had to stay strong. I knew how fucked up this was, but I also knew it was necessary. So I just told Eurus to continue on to Gaia.

We landed on Gaia, near where we'd landed the first time. We planned on using the GPS from the air to find Ares, but Z kept complaining about needing to go to the bathroom.

"I swear I'll piss all over the inside of this ship if you don't land right this second," he said.

After we landed, I activated the GPS function to locate Ares. It said he was pretty far west. I got his coordinates: 38° 17′ 17″ N, 27° 10′ 37″ E. Eurus set the ship's target coordinates accordingly, but right as we were about to take off, we were attacked by three Martians who came out of the woods and started shooting at us, and the ship.

We weren't prepared.

Z got shot in the leg and was down. Eurus and I didn't have our guns ready and had to think fast. Eurus disarmed one of the Martians and broke the guy's neck. He disarmed another one, but this proved to be a tougher fight. I was able to disarm the third and last guy, but he was putting up a fight as well. There we were, Eurus and I fighting two guys hand to hand, while Z was playing dead with a leg wound.

The guy I was fighting slammed me to the ground and began choking me. I thought I was going to die. I tried to get him off of me even as I felt my life slowly ebbing away. The next thing I knew, the guy was pushed off of me somehow. I couldn't see anything until a few seconds later.

I assumed it was Eurus who pushed the guy off, but when I was finally able to get up, Eurus was still fighting his guy. I looked to my left, and there I saw Ella, the giant cat, tearing the guy to shreds.

Eurus and the guy he was fighting noticed her too, and stopped fighting. The guy stared at Ella as she slowly walked toward him, growling louder than any animal I'd ever heard before, blood dripping from her fangs. Eurus's guy turned around and ran off. Ella let loose another vicious growl right before chasing him down, tackling him from behind, and biting into his back, pulling out his spinal cord.

"Gross," said Z, as he slowly got up. Turns out he was barely shot, the bullet just grazing his leg. He was overreacting, as usual.

Bastet, Perses's cat, came running out of the ship at this point, which freaked Ella out for a second. Bastet began rubbing her body up against Ella's legs while meowing over and over again. Once they got used to each other and Ella stopped looking like she was gonna eat Bastet, we got them both in the ship with us and followed the GPS coordinates to Ares's location.

Once we got there, we could see all the Gaians assembled, as if they were at a concert back on Mars. A few spears hit the ship as we landed. I guess they didn't realize it was us. I forgot they had never seen the ship before.

They continued to freak out while we landed and started to open the ship. Finally, I saw Ares walk through the crowd and up to the ship. He started laughing and said some stuff in Gaian to the crowd, and everyone calmed down.

Out of nowhere Eve ran up and hugged me. That was a really nice surprise. Not only was it good to know she was still alive, but it was also an amazing feeling to realize that she must have missed me as much as I'd missed her.

"Don't leave again," she said. Although she spoke with a thick accent, her Martian had improved a great deal.

"I won't," I replied. "Unless you come with me."

"So, what have you guys been up to?" I asked Ares.

"They keep finding us," he replied, "so we have to keep running. We have lost a lot of our people, but we keep finding more to join us as we go."

"Mars is gone," I replied, "so the Martians on Gaia are the only Martians left. If we can kill them all, we will have won. And it will be over."

"Do you have a plan?" asked Eve.

"Yes. Well, sort of. No, not really. But we will figure it out."

"We?" said Z. "Finally giving all of us credit?"

"Wait," said Ares. "Who is that tiny cat standing next to Ella?"

"Oh, yeah. That's Bastet," said Eurus. "She's kind of like our mascot. She watches while Ella fucks shit up."

"What does it mean, to *fuck shit up*?" Eve asked.

"It's what we're about to do to the Martian Army," said Z.

"So, how do we do it? What's next?" asked Ares.

"We keep moving," I said. "Let's make our army even bigger, and let's send some Gaians out to assemble more battalions in other locations."

"Where?" asked Eurus.

Before I could answer, out of nowhere a lone Martian soldier appeared over a hill.

"I come in peace!" he screamed—right before a spear went through his stomach.

Ares and I ran toward the man, who was still alive, but barely.

"Who are you?" I asked.

"Doesn't matter. I need to speak to Adam Jelani. Quickly."

"Uhhh, well, that's me, but what—"

"I know where there are hundreds more Gaians," he interrupted, his voice weak. "In a group similar to this one. I rebelled too, with six other Martians, but they're all dead. My last best chance to save them was to find you. Rumor has it that you killed the king, and lived to talk about it."

"Yeah, that's true," I said. "Where are these hundreds of Gaians?"

"In a cave. The coordinates are thirty-one degrees, forty-five minutes, twenty-one seconds north, thirty-five degrees, one minute, twenty-eight seconds east."

"Are there any other Martians like us anywhere else?"

"No. Not that I know of—or I wouldn't have walked fifteen hundred kilometers to find you."

"Fifteen hundred kilometers?!" I replied. "Fine. Okay. What is your name?"

"Lieutenant Hermes," he said.

Ares stepped closer and said, "You died to save my brothers and sisters. I will forever think of you as my brother as well."

I went back to the group and explained to Eurus and Z that we had to go to the cave to meet up with all of these other Gaians, which would double the size of our army, or more. I asked Eurus to take the ship to the location immediately, so he could ensure their safety. Plus, I knew we wouldn't want to walk all the way back to the ship later.

"I'm supposed to go by myself?" Eurus asked.

"You can take Z with you, if you want," I replied.

"Actually, I wouldn't mind some peace and quiet finally, I'll go by myself."

Ares, Z, and I gathered our troops and started moving southeast after Eurus left, toward the coordinates. This walk is going to take us days, maybe weeks.

We walked until it was dark, then found a place to sleep.

Day 26

I woke up with Eve in my arms, her back to my chest. With all the terrible things going on, the one good thing has been meeting her. If anything were to happen to her, it would be hard for me to continue. I think she will be fine, with Ares and me to protect her. If she does die, that means I will probably be dead, too.

After everyone had woken up, we ate some food, drank some water, and started heading southeast again.

After about five minutes of walking, we were attacked by about twenty Martian guards. Before I could even react, the Gaians had taken care of them.

"Our fighting skills have improved since you left," said Ares. "We have had practice, as this happens a lot."

We kept walking, and kept running into guards. The Gaians would kill them, and unfortunately, a lot of them would die, too. Ares assures me that more Gaians will continue to join us as we move along. They know they are safer in numbers, so most Gaians will see the crowd and join us without even asking or caring what we are doing.

"Why couldn't we all go in the ship with Eurus?" asked Z.

"Because the Gaians wouldn't know how to find us," I said. "And remember, I said he could take you, but he didn't want to."

"That's fucked up," Z replied. "How long is this walk gonna take?"

"I don't know."

"Well, if you had to guess," Z insisted.

"A couple days."

"Like, from now? Or from when we left?"

"From now."

"Damn—are you sure?"

"No, I'm not," I replied. "It's a guess."

We kept going southeast until I noticed that Eurus's coordinates finally matched the target coordinates. We continued walking in his direction until it got dark again, then found a place to sleep. I might not write much, if anything, the next couple days—unless something interesting happens.

Since Mars is gone, I decided to paint it with some berries and leaves. Hopefully no one will forget what it looked like.

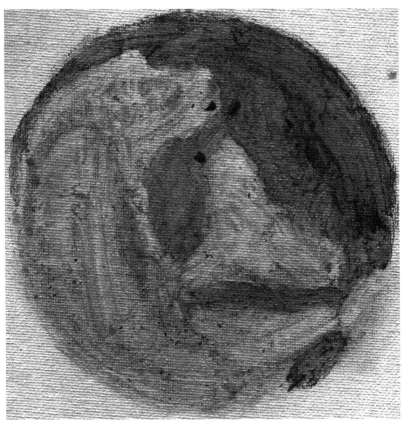

Day 31

Well, we're still not there. We hit water today; I think it's the same sea as before.

"Nice cave," Z said sarcastically, looking at the sea.

"Eurus is still southeast," I said. "Let's just walk along the coast to the east until we can go south again."

"How do you know he's not dead?" Z said.

"He's not. His coordinates keep changing, but not by much. He's probably walking around the area."

"Or something ate him and that's walking around the area." Said Z.

"If something ate him, I doubt it would swallow a GPS whole and have it still work."

"Whatever." Z replied, looking very out of energy; we all were.

We kept going east along the coast, but still inland enough that hopefully if there were any Martian boats, they wouldn't see us.

Again, there's not much to write. We're just walking, I thought I'd at least document that we hit water at 36° 13' 45" N, 29° 55' 12" E and are walking around it. I'll just catch up on everything when we get to Eurus. All this walking is destroying my energy, I can't think straight.

Day 42

Oh my god. I never want to have to walk for that long ever again.

Somehow we made it. Eurus even had food ready for us when we got there. I forgot that he could see our coordinates, too, so he knew we were still alive, and that we were getting close to his location. He had found the cave, which was big enough for all of us to be in, to escape the sun. There weren't many trees around; it looked like the area had already been fully harvested by the Martians. This was both good and bad— bad, because there isn't much food here for us, and good, because the Martians probably won't come back to this spot.

When we first arrived we could hear Eurus yelling *What the fuck?!* We thought something must be wrong. Turns out he was fine; he just saw some crazy-looking bugs. We reacted the same way when we saw them.

What was more interesting was what was already in the cave: about five hundred Gaians, probably the ones Lieutenant Hermes had told us about, giving us a total of about seven hundred now. Ares talked to them; I'm guessing he explained what had happened to Hermes, and that we were here to help them.

After I got hydrated and ate some food, Eve came running up to me.

"Follow me," she said with a smile, and then ran off into the cave.

I followed.

She kept running further into the cave, until we were in an area I hadn't known existed. She turned around really fast and ran up and kissed me. It was a quick kiss, no tongue; she was smiling and giggling.

"I'm sorry," she said, still smiling.

"Don't be," I said, as I started to smile.

"I've been wanting to do that for a long time," she said, jumping up and down.

"Me too," I replied, laughing.

Her smile went away as she lowered her head, then looked back up at me.

"I have a question," she said. "Are you going to win this war? Because I miss how things used to be, before you came here. No offense. I still like you."

"I hope we will," I replied. "But how did things used to be?"

"It was much more beautiful," she said. "No gunshots, no garbage floating in our waters. I only wish it were still beautiful."

"Well, at least you're still beautiful."

Chapter Fourteen
EMBRACE THE MARTIAN

Day 42 Continued

Eve looked at me like she was confused by what I'd said. I realized she was new to the Martian language, but she had just used the word *beautiful*, so I figured she knew what it meant. I'm not sure what the Gaian word for it is, but it seems like maybe she had never been described this way before.

I kept trying to figure out what she was thinking while also trying to decide what to say next. Before I could spit out another word, she pounced on me like Ella had jumped on that Martian soldier.

We were making out when Z walked into our area.

"Yo, I'm gonna hook the TV up to the ship to use for electri—"

He stopped abruptly when he saw us, then smiled. "Oh *shit*. Get it!"

I could still hear him as he walked out, I'm assuming, talking to Eurus. "Yo, he's about to find out if he can have kids with her . . ."

One thing led to another, and you know what happened next. I've never felt like that while being intimate with anyone before—all full of butterflies and shit. Usually, it's just sex. But this time, it was like our souls were entwined. I could feel her energy, and it sure seemed like she could feel mine as well.

Z can talk all the shit he wants, but when I see Eve, I don't see a Gaian. I don't see a Martian, either; I just see a soul. I see a soul that I feel like I've been looking for, for my entire life. I didn't know I was looking for her until I found her. She gives me reason to continue. She gives me belief in the future. She gives me everything, in a world where I have nothing.

When we finally walked out of the cave, Z and Eurus were playing *Motorsport 5*, with everything hooked up to the ship for power. I was impressed that Z had followed through and figured out a way to do that. Ares was watching, never having seen a TV before, let alone a video game. He was pretty into it.

"Yes! Slam him into the wall!" he yelled.

Come to think of it, he's never seen a car either. But whatever, he was enjoying himself.

"Excuse me, Mr. Adam," said a young Gaian. "Are you gonna kill all the Martians?"

"Well, only the bad ones," I said. Then I remembered Hermes, who wasn't bad. To be fair, we hadn't known at the time that there were any good ones, other than us. Now we do, so I've explained to the Gaian soldiers that next time, they should wait before throwing a spear, until we're sure the Martians pose a threat.

If we can get more Martians on our side, we will have a much better chance. We could get a couple more ships, maybe one with some guns on it; that would be pretty useful. Until then, we have three gunmen and an army of spearmen to work with.

The other group of Gaians that were here when we arrived, the ones Hermes had told us about, had not been attacked by Martians. While out hunting they had been pounced on by some kind of animal. Hermes was the only one that had stayed to watch the group. After way too many hours, he went out to look for them and found their torn-apart bodies.

That's what the Gaians here have been telling me, anyway. They said "Struthio" had attacked them, but who knows what the hell that means? Ares didn't know when I asked him. Must be an animal local to this area.

Day 43

After a full day's rest from that ridiculously long walk, today we were actually able to get some planning done. I talked to some of the new Gaians with Ares. I asked if they knew of any other good Martians on Gaia who could become our allies, maybe a group similar to this one. I knew there had to be others somewhere; the question was, did they know where.

"They said the only good Martians they have ever met have been you and the ones they were with before," said Ares.

I'll have to do some searching of my own. Maybe spy on some camps, if I can find any. See if any Martians seem like they don't wanna be there, or are arguing with other guards.

That won't be today, though. I still don't feel like walking anytime soon.

"Ask them if the Martians they were with had any gear we could look through," I said to Ares.

"They do," Ares confirmed.

They had a scanner, which should be able to pick up Martian radio traffic. However, it's pretty shitty; I'm not sure if it even works. We could hear a little bit, but it was hard to make out. This is how they must have heard about Atlantis, and how they knew to head that way to find us. We could possibly find other rebels the same way they did, but we would need to fix up the scanner first, so I went to ask Eurus.

I found him smoking with Z.

"We're gonna run out of that shit eventually," I said.

"Nah," Z replied. "I've been planting this shit all over the place since the day we first landed."

"Word," said Eurus, laughing.

"Plus, I took, like, four pounds from that guy we bought the asclepius from on Mars."

"Wait, what?" I asked.

"Yeah, I robbed that dude," Z replied. "After you guys went inside Perses's house and I ran back out saying I'd forgotten something in his car. He had about four pounds, and I hid it by the ship. I snuck it into the ship while you were talking to Perses. I wanted to surprise you. *Surprise!*"

"Why did you do that?" I asked.

169

"Why the fuck wouldn't I?" Z replied. "We were about to kill everyone there anyway. You guys shoulda stole some shit too."

"Yeah, but you did it, like, three days before we left," I said. "Whatever, Eurus. Can you fix a scanner?"

"Like a computer scanner?" he asked.

"No, a radio scanner."

"I can try."

As a pilot, I'm guessing he probably knows more about radios than either Z or me.

There was also a small arsenal of guns left behind from the previous Martians. We could probably start teaching some Gaians how to use them. Definitely not all of them, though. There are only about twenty guns and a shitload of Gaians. Most importantly, there is a lot more ammo. That was about all they had, besides some personal belongings; nothing that would be useful to us.

Eurus worked on the radio most of the day, and eventually, it sounded like it was working pretty well. We could kinda hear the guards talking to each other, although we weren't sure what they were saying. A lot of it was in code, and it was one Z and Eurus didn't recognize. They must have changed it so the rebels wouldn't know what they're talking about. Smart move on their part, I guess.

"Do you know how far this can reach?" I asked Eurus. "Like, could this chatter be from anywhere on the planet, or is it close by?"

"I would guess probably within sixteen hundred kilometers," he replied. "So it could be from where we were originally—or it could be from somewhere completely different. But it could also be from twenty kilometers away, for all we know."

Hopefully, they aren't that close, but at least we can hear them now.

I saw Eve looking at me with a small smile, playing with the hair on her chest. Which isn't something I ever thought I'd be saying about a girl I'm falling in love with, but there it is. I followed her into the cave again and we kissed, but didn't go much further this time. I told her I'd rather wait until nighttime—that I was too busy right now. This time when I left, Eurus just looked at me with a smirk and shook his head. I'm not sure if it was approval or not, but I don't care.

Z was the only one still listening to the radio, and I heard him yelling for me and Eurus. When we got there we heard some kind of alert. Sirens over the radio, followed by a voice saying *Mars has fallen. I repeat, Mars has fallen.*

So, I guess they just found out. Everyone there must have died instantly, so there was no one to call back to Gaia and tell the Martians what happened. I'm guessing someone left to go back to Mars and got there to see it was all rubble now.

The message over the radio continued: *If you are hearing this, do not leave Gaia unless you have enough fuel to return. Please report to your bases immediately. We need to regroup and begin a new plan of attack against the rebels.*

Repeat: Abandon all camps and return to your assigned bases.

They had said *the rebels*—enough confirmation for me that there's more than just us out there. Or maybe that's just wishful thinking. It was just a few of us that blew up Mars, after all, so it's possible they only *think* there's more of us, when it's really only our small group.

However, I can't let myself believe we are the only Martians left that aren't completely insane.

Day 44

Today, we woke up to an attack. The biggest one I have seen so far. I don't know how they found us, but they did. I grabbed a sniper rifle from the arsenal and started picking off every Martian I could get a shot at from inside the cave. Eurus and Z used assault rifles, and the Gaians attacked with their spears, except for a few that were using guns; I guess they were already trained.

Eve was in the cave with some of the other women and the children. Some women preferred to fight, but all the children were required to stay in the cave.

"This is bullshit!" yelled Z. "Why do they have to attack so early?! I was having a great dream!"

Ares was doing some insane moves. I kept thinking he was about to get himself killed. He was the only Gaian not throwing his spears; instead, he was dual-wielding them and stabbing Martians up close. At one point, there were too many Martians around him and I thought for sure we were going to lose him. I was sniping as many of the Martians around him as I could see, but it was becoming too many.

Suddenly, I noticed through my scope that there was another group of Martians coming from the south. As if this fight didn't already have enough Martians! It was overkill.

I had my scope on the one I assumed was the leader, figuring my best bet would to be kill her and then maybe the others would leave. Although that hadn't worked when I killed the king, I had to try something, or we would all die.

I saw them draw their weapons and I was about to fire, but something was wrong: They weren't looking in the right direction; they were looking at the other Martians, and then they opened fire on them.

It was the rebels.

I yelled to all of the Gaians to get them to pull back. Z and Eurus heard me, realized what was happening, and escorted the Gaians back toward the cave as safely as they could. Some still got shot, but we saved as many as we could.

Z wanted to go back and fight, but I told him it wasn't a good idea right now—not until we knew how to tell who was who.

It didn't take long before the Martians fled, running back the way they'd come.

After the attack was over, we had about five hundred Gaians left. The rebels approached us, and this time I made sure that all the Gaians knew not to kill any of them.

"Which one of you is Adam?" asked the woman I had my scope on. She was taller than most women, with long red hair and dark blue eyes.

"That's me," I replied.

"It is an honor to meet you. I am Commander Gabrielle Bellona," she said, extending her arm to shake my hand.

"Wait—that's really Adam?" asked one of the men with her. "The leader of the rebellion? We actually found him?"

"I'm Adam Jelani," I replied. "I don't know who the leader of the rebellion is."

"Oh, *shit*," said another one. "It really *is* him."

"Apparently you don't know this," said Bellona, "but you are the leader of the rebellion. There are a lot of us that don't agree with what is happening on Gaia, but none of us could do anything about it until you opened our eyes. You showed us that revolt is possible. You started all of this. We wouldn't be here fighting against the Martian Army if you hadn't given us the inspiration to do it. And rumor has it you and your team were also the ones to blow up Mars?"

"Yeahhhh, sorry about that," I said, feeling guilty. "I didn't know what else to do."

"Don't be sorry. It was the only thing *to* do. If you hadn't, we would probably all be dead by now."

I turned around to look at everyone. Z and Eurus were standing to my left and right, and all the Gaians were behind us. Eve looked like she was jealous, probably because there was a Martian woman standing there. She has nothing to worry about; I'd still rather have her.

I looked back at Bellona, "Sooo, what now?" I said.

"Do you have tracking devices in your arms still?" she asked. "I'm guessing you don't, but I have to make sure."

Z and Eurus showed her the scars on their arms that showed where the tracking devices had been removed.

"And what about you, Adam?" she asked.

"I'm not military," I said.

"Really?"

"Uh, really."

"Okay, then. Well, we have a base south of here. We will have ships come and pick up you and your army and transport you there. We will brief you on everything you need to know when everyone is there. The first ship will be here soon. We will stay until the last ship arrives, to make sure your army stays alive."

"Okay, but you have to bring my cats, too," I said, pointing at Ella and Bastet.

"Not a problem."

"And that Gaian," I said, gesturing toward Eve, "she stays with me. Also, these two Martians and the huge, beefy Gaian—we will all go on the last ship with you. I want to make sure the army stays alive, too."

I turned around to pack up what I thought I might need, and Z immediately said, "How do we know we can trust her?"

"She and her team just killed a bunch of Martians," said Eurus.

"Maybe it was fake. They just made it look like that."

"No," Eurus said. "Z, just stop. Let's go. We finally get to go somewhere safe and you wanna question it."

I walked past them and up to Eve.

"Who is she?" she asked.

"I don't know. Her name's Gabrielle Bellona, I guess," I replied.

"I don't like her."

I kissed her and walked into the cave to get my guns and other belongings.

I wasn't sure what to expect of this base. Would it just be another cave? And who was in charge?

While waiting for the ships, Z asked Bellona if he could bring his TV and gaming system.

"We have plenty of TVs and games where we're going," she replied.

Z looked the most excited I've ever seen him, jumping around, yelling, "*YES! YES!* I'm gonna smoke all you guys in every game they *got!*" I'm guessing it must be a pretty nice base, considering it has electricity.

We decided to keep our ship here, since we obviously won't need it anymore.

We waited as the ships arrived and took all the Gaians south. Finally, the last ship came.

"I guess this is our ride," said Z.

"Don't make it weird," said Eurus.

We got on, and found that it was much bigger than our ship, and a lot more luxurious on the inside.

It wasn't that long of a ride. As we lowered to the
ground, I could see that the base was surrounded by a wall.
Inside was a big building, about the size of King Xavier's castle.
There weren't really any other structures, like Atlantis had—
just the one big building and some storage areas, surrounded
by antiaircraft guns and rebel guard patrols.

"How did you guys build this?" I asked.

"It used to be a regular Martian base," Bellona replied.
"We took it over from the inside. It was pretty easy, because we
were already inside the base, and there were more rebels here
than regular Martians. But none of them knew we were rebels.
We didn't even know for sure which ones were rebels and
which ones weren't. We couldn't talk about it much, obviously.
But it worked."

"Why are there so many antiaircraft guns?" Eurus
asked.

"Because of you three. They saw your ship on radar,
and weren't sure what kind it was or if there were any more, so
they installed all of these to be safe."

"How did you find us?" asked Z.

"The same way those other Martians did. The first time
they saw your ship on radar, it disappeared and they were
unable to relocate it. They went to the location but no one was
there. The next time they caught it on radar, it was moving,
and then it disappeared from radar, so they assumed you'd
landed. They were right. They pinpointed your coordinates,
but we took over the base around the same time.
Unfortunately, they had already informed other Martian bases

of your location; everyone was on their way to you. We are lucky we got you out as soon as we did."

Once we'd landed at the base, the ship's door opened, and I walked out first. Martians and Gaians alike were working and living on the base, and they all stopped and looked at me as I walked down from the ship. It was completely silent. Bellona and Eve followed, standing next to me as I looked out into the crowd of people, staring at me.

"Well, say hello," said Bellona. "Shake some hands or something."

"Yo," said Z, from still inside the ship. "Is it safe? Can I come out now?"

"Yeah, man," said Eurus, as he walked out.

Ares walked out last, looking like he was in shock to see a place where his people were being treated as equals by so many Martians. He might have cried a little.

We all walked toward the building, following Bellona. A lot of people looked confused when they saw Ella and Bastet following behind us, but they will just have to get used to them. As we walked by, they all got down on one knee and lowered their heads.

Bellona called on her radio as we were walking.

"This is Operation Star Man," she said. "We have him. On our way to the conference room."

"Damn, this is legit," said Z. "I wonder what kinda food they got here."

We all got to the conference room, where there was a big table with a TV on the wall. Four other rebels were already in the room, waiting for us. The rest of us gathered around the table with them.

"Well, this is Adam," said Bellona. "And his crew."

They just stared at me, waiting for me to say something.

"Uhhh, hello?" I said.

"Hello," they all said.

Then silence again.

"You guys got snacks?" asked Z. "I'm hungry."

"Are you serious?" said Eurus.

"Yeah, I'm serious," Z replied. "You tryin' to say you ain't hungry?"

One of the rebels passed Z a bowl of pretzels, which he dug into. After a moment, Eurus took some as well.

"Okay, Bellona told me you guys had to brief me?"

"Yes, of course," said one of the rebels. "We know where the Martian bases are, but they are all heavily guarded. We need to figure out how to infiltrate them, but we're not sure how."

Z laughed.

"Okay, that wasn't much of a brief," I said. "Which one of you is in charge?"

"You are, King Adam," said one of the men.

Chapter Fifteen
THE NEXT MOVEMENT

Day 44 Continued

Z whispered, "*King Adam?*"

"Umm," I said, "I'm sorry—what?"

"We are our own government now," said Bellona. "We are no longer the Martian military, but we are an army, and this is our kingdom. A kingdom needs a king."

"What if I don't want to be king?" I asked.

"But you do," said Eurus.

"And if you didn't," said Bellona, "we might not have a chance. You are the only one capable of leading us to destroy the Martian Army. You have already been leading an army to do this. The only difference is, now you have about eight hundred and fifty soldiers, two hundred of which are Martians. Now you have your own military base. We've already built a bunk area for your whole army. Plus, you and your friends get your own rooms."

I had them show me the locations of all the Martian bases. They are scattered all around the planet, so obviously we need ships. They also have antiaircraft guns, so we would most likely have to land outside the bases and travel the rest of the way on foot. Some of them are like this one, surrounded by just a wall. Others are caves.

Our location right now is 29° 8′ 36″ N, 29° 25′ 44″ E.

The locations of the other six bases are listed below, in order of distance from us.

Base Molae: 41° 53′ 35″ N, 12° 29′ 56″ E.

(2,079 km away)

Base Eebe: 8° 19′ 33″ N, 47° 52′ 42″ E.

(3,010 km away)

Base Yama: 18° 57′ 47″ N, 72° 55′ 50″ E.

(4,530 km away)

Base Sisimito: 17° 6′ 54″ N, 88°55′ 40″ W.

(11,631 km away)

Base Apache: 32° 49′ 15″ N, 106° 19′ 12″ W.

(11,688 km away)

Base Karora: 24° 39′ 48″ S, 137° 0′ 51″ E.

(12,923 km away)

We weren't sure which one to start with, but that didn't matter yet. First we needed to figure out how we would even take over one base, let alone six.

"Is it possible there might still be Martians at these bases that would join us?" I asked.

"I don't think so," Bellona replied. "Something has changed with them. We try to reason with the ones we know, but they don't seem like themselves anymore."

"How many ships do we have?" I asked.

181

"Just the four you have already seen," said one of the men. "Two gunners and two transport."

"I didn't even know the Martian Army made gunner spaceships," said Eurus.

"Well, they didn't until you guys started causing so many problems. They're essentially just transport ships rigged with guns and missiles."

It would make sense to attack all of the bases at once, similar to what we did with the camps. However, the problem with that is, our army might not be big enough to divide by six and still take down all of these bases. Plus, we did the camps at night; these bases are located all around the planet. It won't be nighttime at all of them at the same time.

We decided it would be best to do one at a time, and each one a little differently.

The first one will be the easiest. We'll just go there and shoot missiles off from a distance and blow that shit up, then have the army run in to clean up. The second one, they will be more prepared. They will probably see the ships from a distance and shoot us down . . .

So we're not really sure yet. We will figure it out tomorrow, I hope.

So, yeah, it's been a super-long day. But they have me in a king-size bed with Eve and a TV and shit, so I'm more relaxed than I have been in a very long time. We even have our own bathroom with one of those tubs with jets. I had Eve try it.

"I feel like I'm in a volcano," she said, smiling.

"Yeah—don't do this in a volcano, though."

"I know, silly. I'm not *stupid*."

"I knowww," I replied. "I was just sayin'."

"Is this what Martians use to get clean?"

"Yeah, or a shower."

"And that hair cream stuff?"

"Yeah, shampoo," I said.

Eve got all cleaned up, with soap and shampoo and everything. It was the first time I had seen her *that* clean. She had always bathed in natural water sources, which I was getting used to doing myself.

"Do I look beautiful?" she asked.

"You already did, but you do smell better." I said with a smile.

She punched my arm.

I got cleaned up too, and now we're going to bed. Another big day tomorrow.

I haven't tried to draw anything in a while, so here's a shitty drawing of my view of the base as we landed.

Day 45

Today, I got the army to work on building more defenses. Once
we start attacking, it won't take them long to figure out where
we are and attack back. We need to be ready. Yes, we're
already pretty equipped with antiaircraft guns and an army,
but they still have a much bigger army and much more ships
and firepower.

Also, blowing up the first base with missiles isn't the
plan anymore. We want to save as much of the base as
possible, so we can take it over and use it as our own.
Obviously, we will have a better chance if we have more bases.

For our first mission, we've decided to attack the base
closest to us, Base Molae, (2,079 kilometers to the northwest).
We will then continue to attack the next ones out, working our
way to those farthest away.

For the first attack, we will have to send someone in.
Not at night; it will be light out when the guards at that base
are doing their normal rounds. We will wait for them to leave
the base as a group and then return. Then, our Martian will
sneak into the group and walk into the base with them,
hopefully unnoticed. It will have to be a pilot, but not Eurus.
Eurus and Z stay with me now, also treated like royalty. So are
Eve and Ares, which is pretty amazing to see. They both wear
full Martian clothing now.

Anyway, once the pilot is inside the base, he will get
into one of their gunner ships and start bombing the areas
where there are Martians. He will also do his very best to avoid
damaging any equipment. Once he has killed enough Martians,

some of our army will then storm in to clean up, leaving most of our soldiers back at the original base to defend against any possible attack.

Eurus and Z were in the conference room when I went over this plan. As soon as we left, Eurus asked, "What if I want to be the pilot that infiltrates the base?"

"You don't," I responded. "The pilot that does this is probably going to get shot down and killed; we just have to hope he kills enough Martians before that happens."

"Damn."

"Can I be king of the next base?" asked Z.

I ignored the question.

They have no bases on the planet other than these six, at least as far as Bellona knows, so if we can successfully take these over, then we will have won. It will be over. There might still be some loose Martian soldiers running around somewhere, but at that point they will have no choice but to join us.

I gathered all of our army into one area outside for a meeting. Over a loudspeaker, I described the plan for the first base. I even made sure to include the part about how the pilot has a pretty good chance of getting shot down and killed.

"Is there anyone with pilot experience brave enough for this job?" I asked.

It was silent for a few seconds. Then one voice said, "I will do it." A woman stepped forward, on the shorter side, and with light blue eyes and medium length blonde hair.

"And what is your name?" I asked.

185

"Captain Astrid Proserpina," she replied.

"Are you sure you want to do this, Captain Proserpina?" I asked.

"Yes."

"You will have till the end of the day to change your mind, if you choose to," I explained. "But tomorrow morning, we leave for Base Molae."

I turned around and walked back to the building with Eurus, Z, Ares, and Bellona. Eve stays inside most of the time now, out of harm's way, with Ella and Bastet.

It is the end of the day now, and Proserpina has not said anything about changing her mind. So tomorrow, it begins.

Day 46

I sounded the alarm to wake everyone up and report to the open area near the entrance to the base. I stood at the podium with Z and Eurus by my side.

"Okay," I said. "A lot of you are gonna die today."

"Way to start off the speech," whispered Z.

"But this is so a lot more of us can live. It is so we can build a free world, where no one is a slave. Where anyone can raise a family, and live in peace. I wish I could say we will finish it today, but that speech is for another day. However, we are close. I guess you could say, today is the beginning of the end. No matter which way it goes, it is going to be the end of them, or it is going to be the end of us. Our ships are ready, and I need them filled. Anyone who's left will stay here and defend against possible attacks.

"We will land eight kilometers away from Base Molae and walk as close as we can without being seen," I continued. "Then, Proserpina will continue on her own. When the army sees that ship go up, you storm in. I will be there with you."

"Whoa, what?" asked Eurus. "Why not stay here?"

"Because. I don't know. I'm trying to be honorable or whatever," I said.

"Well, there are still five bases left after this one; how is the army gonna know what to do without you?"

"I didn't say I would die," I replied. "I've survived this long."

"I don't think you should go," said Eurus. "It's too much of a risk."

"Fine," I said.

Everyone was looking at us awkwardly. They couldn't hear us because we weren't talking into the mic.

"Never mind," I said. "I won't be there. But the army does need a leader. Proserpina already volunteered to be the pilot; would anyone else like to volunteer to lead the army into battle?"

"Yeah. I'll do it," said Bellona, pushing past us and speaking into the mic.

"Okay. Well, let's get started then," I said. "Bellona— choose your soldiers and fill all four ships. After they're filled, those who are left will start to patrol the base."

It didn't take long at all. Proserpina and a couple hundred other Martians and Gaians filled the ships, about fifty units per ship.

I had to have one more quick talk with Bellona before they left.

"Okay," I said, "run me through the plan. I trust you; I just have to make sure you got this down. I won't be there. I need to know it will be done right."

"We're gonna land eight kilometers out," she replied. "Head as close to the base as we can without being seen. Then, Proserpina continues on her own to join a group of Martians entering the base. When we see the ship go up and start attacking the base, we storm in."

"Great." I said. "Probably *way* easier said than done, but I trust you'll get it done. Return safely, please. And with as much of the army as possible. Try to recruit new people if there is anyone left alive."

"Of course, my king."

I walked back toward Z and Eurus.

"What should I do now, my king?" said Z sarcastically.

"Shut up," I said, as Eurus laughed.

We didn't use radios for this attack, not even ones programmed for two-way communication. We couldn't risk having them get on the frequency and finding out we were coming. They would just kill Proserpina as soon as she showed up.

It's getting late. I wish I could write more and tell you what is going on with the battle, but I'm not there. However, if and when they return, I will make sure to get all the details and write about it tomorrow.

If they don't return, I'm not sure I'll know what to do.

Day 47

Last night, after I was done writing, I sat up on the roof of the base with Eurus and Z. We just smoked, waiting for the army to return.

"Yo," said Z, "remember when we first met?"

"Of course," I said.

Z looked up to the sky and said, "You was just some dude, trying to get into the MIPE building. Said you was gonna steal a fuckin' spaceship. I was like, 'Damn, this dude is *out* of his *fuckin'* mind.' To tell you the truth, I went with you expecting to die."

"What do you mean?" asked Eurus.

"Things were going pretty terrible for me," he replied. "I got into the drug game because of my parents. They decided to start making mania in our basement. I was five at the time, and they taught me how to do it, and made me help. They got locked up when I was nine, which meant I was forced into the military. I started working with Hades because I needed to make more money somehow; the army didn't pay enough. That was going to be my life forever. Until you came up with this crazy fuckin' idea, Adam. I figured it would be a really badass way to die, trying to leave Mars in a spaceship. I knew if I didn't die, it would be a pretty badass story. And here I am. I never expected we would get this far."

"Yeah, it's pretty fuckin' crazy," I said.

"I had a feeling it could escalate to this," said Eurus. "Just didn't think I'd live long enough to see it."

"Well, you did," said Z. "All three of us did. Just a few mothafuckin' Martian gangstas."

"Out to take over the world," added Eurus.

"And if we can't take it over," I said, "destroy it and build a new one."

"And that we have," said Z.

He was right. We're not done yet, but he was still right. Mars is gone, so as far as I'm concerned, we've already won. Even if the remainder of the Martian Army manages to kill us all, they can never change what we have already accomplished.

"By the way, guys," I said. "I think we have to start saying our ages differently. A year on Mars is one point eighty-eight years on Gaia—which means I'm actually twenty-three."

"Me too," said Eurus.

"And I'm twenty-six. Damn, that's weird," said Z.

We kept talking, exchanging stories until the sun started to come up. We figured we should probably try to get some sleep. As we stood up, I saw the best thing I've seen since this all started. Well, second best, behind Eve.

Over the horizon, six Martian ships appeared. The three of us ran down through the building and out into the ship landing area as the six ships drew closer and landed: all four of our ships, plus two new gunners. They were nice gunners, different from the two we already had. They didn't look like converted transport ships, but rather purpose-built gunners.

When the first of the new gunners landed and opened its door, I was shocked when I saw Proserpina walk out. She was still alive.

"Oh my god," I said. "You didn't get shot down."

"Actually, she did," said Bellona, walking out from one of the other ships. "But that didn't stop her. She got out of the ship and ran right toward another one, got in, and kept attacking."

"Damn, now that's luck," said Z.

"No," said Bellona. "If it happened once it would be luck, but she was shot down again, and got on another ship. It's not luck at all—it's skill."

"I . . . umm . . ." Eurus hesitated while looking at Proserpina.

"You, umm, what?" she asked.

"You wanna go for a drink sometime?" he said.

She laughed. "I might have some champagne we could use to celebrate," she said. "Come on." They walked into the building together.

"Why'm I the only one not gettin' any?" asked Z. Then he looked at Bellona, "Ayo—"

"Not interested," she said, cutting him off.

"I was just gonna ask if you'd recruited anyone new. Damn," he said.

"No," she replied. "Well, sorta. There are six unconscious Martians in that ship there," she said, pointing to the farthest one. "Maybe when they wake up, someone could convince them to be new recruits. *If* they wake up."

"What's wrong with them?" I asked.

"They were too close to some of the explosions, I'm guessing; not too sure. But they were the only ones left alive when it was all over, so we took them with us."

"All right. Umm . . . well, I guess you could put them in the dungeon until they wake up? Wait, do we have a dungeon?"

"We do," said Bellona.

"Okay, put them in there and have a doctor check on them once in a while. Have one check them out now, too."

"We only have one real doctor," she said. "Dr. Andre Agwu. He's young, but he's still the best doctor I've ever met. I'll get him on it."

That's when I finally got some sleep, even though the sun was already up.

I woke up around 1200 to Ella licking my face.

Eve was in the tub again. I tried to join her, but she said she wasn't in the mood.

I went to the dungeon to check on the prisoners. I found them all awake, but vomiting on the floor.

"What the *fuck?!*" I exclaimed.

One of them looked at me and said, "Get away from us." He tried to say more, but began vomiting again.

I walked around the building looking for Dr. Agwu. When I finally found him running through the hallway, I stopped him and said, "The prisoners are throwing up all over the place."

"Yeah, a lot of people are," he replied. "The prisoners were part of a biological warfare attack."

I felt stupid for not thinking of that as a possibility.

"Who else is sick?" I asked.

"About thirty Gaians; no Martians," Dr. Agwu said. "Other than the ones in the dungeon."

"Is it deadly?" I asked.

"Yeah," he replied. "We've lost three already."

"Fuck," I said. "Where are the infected Gaians?"

"Quarantined, in the room at the end of this hall. Apologies, my king, but I must get back to work. If you see anyone with symptoms of the death flu—the only confirmed manifestation is vomiting—please send them to me."

I went out to the front where the rest of the army was patrolling or building defenses. I found Bellona to ask her a few questions.

"Hey, sorry if I was confusing last night or whatever," I said. "I was mostly asleep and a little high."

"I didn't notice," she replied. "I assumed you were always like that."

"Like what?" I asked.

"High."

"Oh, no. I wish. But anyway, how does Base Molae look now? Could we use it?"

"A lot of it would have to be rebuilt," she replied. "I can send a team over there to rebuild if you would like."

"Umm, yeah. Is that a good idea, you think? Or will the Martians be sending troops there?" I was still unsure about how to make these huge decisions. Bellona seemed to know this, and was helping a lot.

"We should wait a little while, maybe a day or two. If they send troops there, they'll do it right away, so we can check in a few days."

"Okay, sounds awesome," I replied. "But we still have to attack the next base, and we're losing Gaians."

"Yes, but they're quarantined, and it's only thirty," she replied. "It might sound heartless, but we can still succeed, even with thirty fewer Gaians. Our army is still about seven hundred and fifty units."

"Why do you think it only infected Gaians?" I asked.

"I don't know," she replied. "Maybe they have a weaker immune system. The Martians in the dungeon were probably injected with something, where the Gaians probably just got it from contact."

"That's weird," I said. "Well, I guess we should move forward and attack the next-closest base, which is Eebe." (Base Eebe is 3,010 kilometers to the southeast)

"Okay," she said. "That one is a series of caves, so we might need a different approach. Plus, Base Molae may have warned the other bases of our plan, so the maneuver with Proserpina won't work."

"Do you have any ideas that *will* work?" I asked.

"We just raid it," she said. "With as much of our army as we can."

"So we just run up on them and start fucking shit up?"

"Yeah, for lack of a better term." She smiled slightly, for the first time. "Unless you come up with something better."

"Okay. Where are Z and Eurus?" I asked.

"Z was in the cafeteria last I saw. And I haven't seen Eurus, or Proserpina. I'm guessing they're still in her room."

"What about Ares?"

"I haven't seen him," she replied.

"Okay, well let me know if you do."

I went to the cafeteria to find Z sitting at a table, alone, stuffing his face.

"Yo, they can make anything here," he said. "When I asked what they had, I was just fuckin' with them, and said, 'I want bacon cupcakes.' But check this shit out. Mothafuckin' bacon cupcakes."

"Gross," I said. "Hey, I need your help."

"With what?" He didn't stop eating the cupcakes.

"Drugs."

"I still got plenty of asclepius. How much you want?"

"You used to sell harder stuff back on Mars, right?"

"You mean, like, kratos?" he asked.

"No. Harder."

"The fuck you want anything harder than that for?" he asked, looking concerned.

"The next Martian base is a cave. And I want to gas it," I replied.

"Ohhhhh, so you want me to be a chemist now?"

"Well, can you do it, or not? I can ask someone else."

"What kind of effects do you want this gas to have?"

"Make them unconscious for at least, like, six hours. Or paralyzed. Or both."

"*Damn*, you want some good shit."

I just stared at him, waiting for an answer.

"I guess I could make such a thing," he said. "How big is the cave?"

"Well, from what I've heard, it's not just one big cave, it's a bunch of smaller ones, so we would need to gas all of them—but I'd guess about sixty thousand square feet in total. Give or take."

"Okay, I need supplies, and I have no idea where to find any of it."

"Hey!" I yelled to some of the Martian chefs in the kitchen.

"Yes, my king?" they said, fast-walking toward me.

"Where do you get this food?" I asked.

"You know, around," responded one of the chefs. "We've been doing it since we first landed here, before the revolution started. We know all the spots to get real meat. It's Gaian animal meat, like Gaian pigs and stuff."

"I don't care about the meat; what about herbs?" I asked.

"Yeah, we can get all that too," they replied, nodding. "Anything, really."

"Great. This guy here, the guy eating the bacon cupcakes?"

"Yes?"

"You are to get him everything he needs," I ordered. "He will make a list for you."

"Yes, my king."

"There," I said to Z. "Now just make a list of everything you need."

"You're really starting to enjoy this king thing, huh?"

I chuckled while I walked away.

Next, I went to Proserpina's room and knocked on the door. There was no answer, so I knocked louder. I could hear rustling, the sound of belt buckles and things of that nature.

Finally, Eurus opened the door, sweaty and out of breath.

"What's good?" he asked.

"I'm gonna need you or your girlfriend to drop gas bombs into a cave," I replied.

"First off, she's not my girlfriend."

"*What?*" I heard her say from inside the room.

"And second, what the hell do you mean by a gas bomb?" he asked.

"A bomb with toxic gas in it," I explained.

"What about the antiaircraft guns?" he asked.

"I don't know yet. I'm thinking maybe we make it in the form of a missile instead of a bomb, so it can be shot from a distance. But we would have to make sure all the alcoves of the cave are hit."

"All right. Well, let me know."

I went back to talk to Bellona to discuss this gas bomb plan with her.

"So what do we do after they're all knocked out?" she asked.

"We disarm all of them, bring them back here, and lock them up," I explained. "Then force them to join us, or die."

"If they choose to join us, how do we know they will stay loyal?" she asked. "They might just say it so they don't get killed, then turn on us later."

"We will give them a test. I'm not sure what kind yet."

I went back to my room to check on Eve. When I opened the door, Ares was there; he looked worried. I then heard Eve vomiting into the toilet.

"She has it?" I asked. Ares looked too broken to respond.

I ran to the quarantine room to find Dr. Agwu, but the room was empty. I found him walking out of the bathroom.

"Where are the patients?" I asked.

"None of them made it, except one of the men in the dungeon," he replied. "I did everything I could, but at least the virus is gone now. The man in the dungeon doesn't appear to have symptoms anymore."

They were all dead.

Realizing Eve was probably going to die too, I was trying hard not to pass out.

"I need you to check on Eve—immediately," I ordered.

"The queen? What's wrong with her?"

"I think she has it," I said. I started to get dizzy, and my eyes were tearing up.

Dr. Agwu and I ran to my room, where Eve was still throwing up over the toilet.

"Give me a little time to examine her," he said. "I'll let you know when we're done."

I waited in the living area of my room, watching an old Martian movie with Ares until finally, Dr. Agwu came to talk to us.

I stood up as soon as I saw him. "Does she have it? Can you help her?"

"She is going to be fine," he replied. "Well, hopefully. I will have to keep checking on her."

"She doesn't have the death flu?" asked Ares.

"Nope," said Dr. Agwu. "She's just pregnant."

Chapter Sixteen
FORBIDDEN FRUIT

Day 47 Continued

Ares looked much happier and hugged both me and Dr. Agwu, hurting my ribs.

"*Family!*" he yelled.

I didn't know how to react to this news.

Yes, I had been dreaming of someday starting a family with Eve, but I'm not sure if now is the best time . . . I guess that doesn't matter at this point, as it's happening now, whether it's a good time or not.

I'm with her now, and we're going to try and get some sleep.

Day 48

When I woke up, Eve seemed to be feeling better, at least for now.

I went to the cafeteria to look for Z. I found him in the back room of the kitchen, barking orders at the men and women who've been gathering supplies for him.

"No!" he yelled. "It needs to be *fresh* and *green!* This shit looks like a caterpillar has been eating it for a *month!* Come on, guys."

"Sir, it's poisonous," said one of the men. "I doubt anything was eating it for very long."

"Well, it looks *fucked up*. Get full leaves, not this rotting shit."

"How's it going?" I asked Z.

"It's whatever; they gave me shitty leaves."

"Does it matter?" I asked, examining the leaves. "They should still have the poison in them, right?"

"Yeah," he replied. "But I'm trying to do the best job possible. This is *my* time to shine."

"Okay, then. How much longer, do you think?"

"Depends. Do you expect me to make the bombs? Or just the poison?"

"Just the poison. I'll make the bombs," I clarified.

"Then it should be done by tomorrow," he said. "But it will have to be tested."

"You can test it on the man in the dungeon if you want."

I went down to the dungeon to talk to the one prisoner who actually survived the death flu.

"Biological warfare?" I asked him. "Seriously? How did you even know we would be there?"

"Apologies," he replied. "But I don't remember anything. I don't even know who I am."

The Martians must have not only infected these prisoners with the flu, but also wiped their memories. Just in case they lived, we wouldn't be able to get any answers from them.

I thought maybe if we gave it some time, his memory would restore eventually. We can't test poison on someone who doesn't even know what is going on. What if Z made it too strong and it kills the guy? He could be on our side for all we know, so I can't let that happen.

I had started to walk out of the dungeon when I heard him ask, "Are you going to kill me?"

I turned around and said, "No. As long as you won't kill us."

"Why would I do that?"

"Well, you have been doing it for a long time now," I replied. "You and the Martian Army. We are a rebel militia, fighting back against the Martians. You can join us, but I want to wait until you at least remember who you are."

"What if I choose to not join you? I don't even know who the good guys are. I don't remember anything."

"Yeah, exactly," I replied. "That's why we're waiting."

"What if I remember, but still don't join you?" he asked.

"Then, yes," I said.

"Yes, what?"

"I *will* kill you."

As I was leaving, I ran into Ares.

"I want to help take over a base," he said. "When do I get to fight?"

"Well, no offense, but I'm worried you might die," I replied. "They have a lot of guns. You would've died if Bellona hadn't saved us."

"Thousands of my people are dying in this war," he said. "Please, allow me the honor of risking my life with them."

"Only if you'll allow me to teach you how to shoot a gun first," I said.

"Those things are loud and annoying."

"I think the guns we took from the guards in the dungeon have silencers. You could use one of those."

"Fine," he said. "Give me one of your magic pebble throwers with a quieting tool."

"Come on," I said. "I'll go grab it right now and we can go outside and practice."

Once we were outside, we walked to a tree stump behind the base and put an apple on it. Then we walked about fifty yards away and looked back.

"Now, I will walk you through how to shoot the apple," I said.

First I made sure he was holding the gun properly, which took a while. Once he finally got that down, I told him to line up the sights on the front and back of the gun. I could have just had him use a scope, but I felt more comfortable having him learn this way first.

"Okay," he said, "I am aiming at the apple."

"Okay. Now gently pull the trigger.'

TFT!

The silenced rifle shot one shot as it pushed against Ares's shoulder very hard. He wasn't expecting that. He missed the apple, but he started laughing and exclaimed, "I love this! It makes me feel powerful and safe."

"Well, let's keep doing it," I said. "It's an automatic—just keep aiming at the apple and hold the trigger down. I want to see how well you can handle the recoil."

TFT TFT TFT TFT TFT!

Ares shot while the bullets rained all over the tree stump and apple, until the apple fell off and he just kept shooting. All I heard was the silencer going off, over and over again, the sounds of bullets hitting shit and Ares laughing maniacally.

"HA HA HA HA HA!! Yes!! I am the super Gaian!! Dieeeeeeeeeee!!"

Finally he stopped while I looked at him awkwardly and said, "Uhh, yeah—so you handled the recoil pretty well. I think that might be enough training for one day."

"Can I keep the gun?" he asked.

"Umm, why don't I hold on to it for now?"

"Okayyyy," he said, clearly disappointed.

For the rest of the day, I mostly just walked around checking on our army and making sure they were doing everything according to plan. With all of these other bases against us, we can never have enough defenses; thus, we are constantly patrolling and building more walls, attack towers, and antiaircraft guns. We have several machinists leading this part of the operation, hand-forging most of the parts, although we do have a welder and some other basic fabrication tools. We've tested the antiaircraft guns they've built, and so far, most of them work.

At the end of the night, I finally had some alone time with Eve. We weren't able to talk much last night, as she just wanted to sleep. However, we did get a chance to tonight.

"You got me pregnant," she said.

"I thought you were going to die," I replied.

"I am," she said. "Eventually—unless I'm immortal and I don't know it. That would be cool."

"I mean, I thought you had the death flu," I explained.

"I don't know what that is, but it sounds scary."

I forget she doesn't know too much about what goes on outside of this room. I don't tell her to stay here; I just tell her to stay in the building. She chooses to stay in the room, mainly watching Martian movies and eating ice cream. I guess that's a good thing. If she'd left this room, she might have actually gotten the flu.

After talking for a while, I started writing this entry.

"What are you going to do when that thing is done?" she asked.

"The journal?" I replied.

"Yeah."

"Well, it's not done until we're done," I explained. "And when that happens, I'll probably bury it for future generations to find."

Day 49

This morning, I walked to the cafeteria to look for Z. He wasn't there. I asked some of the chefs if they knew where he'd gone.

"I'm not sure," one of them said. "We were just glad he finally left."

"He said something about testing the poison," said another.

I ran down to the dungeon, since I remember telling him he could test it on the prisoner. I'd forgotten to tell him to hold off on that until the man's memory restores. But then again, we need to act fast. It does need to be tested first, or we could be making the trip to Base Eebe for nothing.

I got down there and found Z passed out on the floor.

The prisoner, still behind bars, looked at me and said, "Yeah, he had a vial of some liquid and said it was my 'lucky day' or something. He opened the top, smelled it for some reason, and now, here we are."

I checked his vitals and he seemed okay to me, but I needed Dr. Agwu to check him out, to be sure.

Once I'd located the doctor and brought him to the dungeon, he confirmed that Z was fine, just unconscious. So I guess it works—as long as Z wakes up.

I didn't want to sit around waiting for that, so I went to the work area and started constructing the missiles.

About an hour later, Dr. Agwu came to me to tell me that Z had woken up. He was resting in the sick bay.

I went to see him, and he said, "Damn, that's some *good shit!*"

"When did you go down there to test the poison?" I asked him.

"Like, 1100," he responded. "It works! I didn't mean to test it on myself, but it works. I actually did it!"

"Uh, well kinda. It's 1300. You were only out for two hours."

"The prisoner said I just smelled it a little. Maybe when the missiles turn it into gas, it will be more effective?" he said, sounding less sure of himself.

"Maybe, but we have to assume it won't."

"I can make a new batch," Z suggested.

"No," I said. "I wanna get this started now. There's no time. Why they haven't started attacking us already is beyond me."

I left Z to rest a bit longer on his cot, and went back to making the missiles.

If the gas only knocks them out for about two hours, we'll have to act much more quickly than we'd previously planned. The missiles will explode on impact, only causing minor injuries—unless a missile hits someone straight in the face or something. After exploding, it will discharge gas into the air that will knock them out immediately. Our troops will then need to load the knocked-out guards into the ship and bring them back here, where they will be held prisoner and given the choice to either join us, or not. Meanwhile, we will have some of our soldiers working on turning Base Eebe into a second base for us.

I went to find Ares and tell him about our next mission.

"I could use your help," I said, smiling. I felt comfortable sending him, because the guards should all be knocked out, and Eurus would be with him.

"Can I practice shooting the gun more today?" he asked.

I'd already intended to let him practice more, so had his gun with me. He looked as happy as a child when I handed it over to him. I let him practice without me this time, trusting that he wouldn't do anything stupid.

"Hey," I said to Bellona, as I walked by her. "We need to figure out where we are putting all these guards after they're captured. Our dungeon won't be big enough. We need to build some kind of massive cell or something."

"We have some pretty big storage rooms we don't really need," she replied. "We could clear them out and keep them in there."

"Okay—can you get some people working on that? And make sure the doors and everything can be one hundred percent secured," I said. "Oh, and I have Ares out back practicing with a gun I gave him. Can you check on him once in a while? He should be fine. I just want to make sure."

"Of course," she said, smiling.

I went to check on Eve. I wish I could spend more time with her, especially now that she's pregnant with my child. I apologized to her and she responded with, "I understand. You are doing what you have to do." She smiled and said, "I still get to be with you at night."

After spending some time with her, I worked through the night, making missiles.

Tomorrow, the attack on Base Eebe will begin.

Day 50

As soon as I got up, I went to wake Eurus to make sure he'd be ready.

Considering I hadn't seen much of him since he and Proserpina had gone to her room, I figured that's where he'd be. I had to knock on her door about eight times before Eurus finally answered.

"What's good?" he asked.

"Are you two ready?"

". . . for?"

I sighed and said, "You are bombing Base Eebe today. Like, in a couple hours."

"Word? All right . . . we will be down by the ships in, like, twenty minutes."

I waited by the ships with the fifteen people I'd chosen to go on this mission, including Ares and Bellona. Once Proserpina and Eurus had come strolling in, it was time to tell everyone what exactly we would be doing.

"Okay," I said, "this is the plan. There will be two ships—one piloted by Eurus, one by Proserpina. One of you will have a gunner ship, and the other, a transport ship. I don't care which one of you pilots which. However, the gunner will head in first and target each of the alcoves of the cave. You will send a missile to each one, and it will discharge a gas that will knock the Martians out. It's important that you hit all of them at the same time, so no guards will be alerted fast enough to put on gas masks.

"As soon as those missiles hit," I continued, "the transport ship will land and you will all storm out, with the exception of Eurus and Proserpina. You will take every single guard you find and put them back in the ship. If there isn't enough room, we will put some of them in the gunner. Although there are just fifteen of you, Bellona says there could be up to sixty people at this base and you have to get them all into that ship in less than a half-hour, making sure you disarm them first. And don't forget to check for hidden weapons, as well."

Eurus looked like he was kind of spacing out, until Proserpina nudged him and told him to pay attention. Ares was smiling, probably happy to be finally going on a mission, while Bellona stood next to him; very serious with her arms crossed.

"I understand it will be cramped in the ship, but the prisoners will all be knocked out, so you can walk on them for all I care. You will get them back here immediately and put them into the storage room Bellona has cleared out and secured. We need to get them there before they wake up. We assume they will wake up two hours after they are knocked out, but that's only based on one test, so we want to try to get it done in an hour or less, to be safe."

"How does the targeting on the gunner ship work?" asked Eurus. "I mean, how are we gonna be able to shoot, like, ten missiles at the same time?"

"A computer screen will enable you to see exactly where to lock on to each alcove separately, then hit launch," I responded. "The missiles will launch two at a time, but it will be really fast, getting through all ten quick enough. So, who is taking which ship?"

They looked at each other, then looked back at me.

Eurus said, "I'll take the gunner; she will take the transport."

"Okay, Proserpina. Here's your crew," I said.

"You're staying here, right?" Eurus asked, looking at me.

"Yes," I said. "But not because of the danger. This mission should be fairly easy, with little to no risk. I am only staying here because the people here might need me. Again, there will be no radio contact between us. I will expect you back in two hours or less."

"And if we aren't back in two hours?" asked Proserpina.

"We come looking for you," I replied. "If the prisoners wake up, even after you disarm all of them, they might be able to take the ship down. There will be a lot more of them than there are of you. It should only take about twenty minutes each way, so if it's been two hours, we have to assume the prisoners have woken up. At that point, it becomes a rescue mission."

They left at 0900, and I went to hang out with Eve while I had the time. I spent about an hour with her, just talking about our future.

"Should we think of a name yet?" I asked her.

"No, we should name it after it's born," she replied. "Once we know if it's a boy or a girl."

Eventually, I decided to go watch the horizon again, and I thought I'd take Z with me.

I found him in the kitchen, of course. But this time he wasn't eating weird-ass food; he was still working on the poison.

"You know they already left with the missiles, right?" I asked him.

"Yeah. I'm making a better batch for next time."

"How do you know I'll wanna use the same plan again?"

"I don't," Z said. "I was bored because you didn't give me anything else to do, and they don't have any good video games here. I figured I'd just keep doing this."

"You wanna go smoke on the roof with me and wait for the crew to come back?" I asked.

"Sir, yes, sir."

We sat up there, smoking and talking. After an hour and a half, I started to get worried. I knew two hours was the deadline, but I'd thought they would be quicker. Luckily, about five minutes later, we spotted the ships over the horizon.

We ran down to the landing area, just in time to see the soldiers from the transport ship unloading the knocked-out guards and transporting them to the storage room on stretchers.

"Easy, right?" I asked Eurus.

"Not exactly," he replied. "There was one alcove we didn't know about."

"Wait—what?"

"We were loading the unconscious Martians into the ship when suddenly six more came out of nowhere. There must have been an extra secret alcove."

"So what happened?" asked Z.

"I guess you didn't notice, but our little battalion of fifteen is now just thirteen."

"Oh, shit," I said, "Did anyone kill those six Martians?"

"Ares did," Eurus replied. "He was closest to them. But they killed two of our soldiers before he could kill them. I guess it could have been a lot worse."

"But it wasn't," I said.

"That's all you're gonna say?"

"Yeah. We still have a lot to do. We don't have time to be worrying about what *could* have happened. Plus, those six Martians probably called for backup before they ran out, so I bet the base is not empty, meaning we can't send our people there."

"At least we have about sixty prisoners," said Eurus.

"Yeah," said Z. "Hopefully we can get some of them to fight for us."

I suddenly remembered the other prisoner we already had in the dungeon. I hadn't checked on him in a while, so I went down there with Eurus and Z.

I looked at the prisoner and asked, "You remember anything yet?"

"Yup," he replied. "And I am very willing to join you."

That was too easy, I thought.

"I don't trust him," said Eurus.

"Let's feed him to the dogs," said Z.

"We don't have any dogs," I said.

"Then we feed him to Ella," said Eurus.

"Tempting, but no," I said. "I need answers from him. And who knows—maybe he's not lying."

"I can hear you guys," he said. "And I'm not lying. Listen, my name is Commodore Glycon, and you can trust me. Most Martians want to join you. They just don't know where to find you, and wouldn't be able to leave if they tried. Zeus knows where everyone is, including you. And he—"

"Back up," I said. "Who the fuck is Zeus?"

"Oh, that's right. You guys are out of the loop, being rebels and all. Zeus is the real king. The king of kings. The god of gods. He has a lot of names."

"Umm . . . so he took over after Horus? Or after Xavier?"

"Horus and Xavier were just puppets. Well, that's what Zeus says, anyway. Most of us believe Xavier was the real king, and Zeus is just saying that it's always been him, to make himself seem more powerful than he really is."

"So where is he?" asked Z.

"No one really knows," said Glycon. "Anyway, as I was saying, Zeus knows where you are. Haven't you wondered why he hasn't had his army attack your base yet? Because he's afraid they would choose to join you. His power is strong, nonetheless; somehow, I feel like he is still managing to control us."

"So, they all want to join us?" I asked.

"No. Not all. But most."

I looked at Z and Eurus, then back at Glycon. "So those sixty prisoners we just got—we didn't kidnap them, we rescued them?"

"Precisely," said Glycon.

"Okay, come with us," I said. "I'm gonna put you with all the other prisoners, or refugees, or whatever they are."

Glycon and I went to the storage room while Eurus and Z went off to work on other projects.

It had been a few hours, so I figured they would all be awake by now. An intercom had been installed so I could talk to them without going in. Unfortunately there was no window or other opening, so I couldn't see them. Guess we didn't think of that.

I spoke into the intercom.

"This is Adam Jelani. I'm in charge of things here, and want you to know you are safe; Zeus cannot see you here. I am going to open the door now. Don't do anything stupid, or you will be shot."

I opened the door. At first glance, I thought they were all still knocked out. But they were wide awake. On their knees, bowing to me.

"You really don't have to do that," I said.

They stood up slowly.

"Will it be this easy to get the rest of you on my side?" I asked.

"No," said one of the men. "Zeus will find a way to make it more difficult."

"How?"

"We're not sure, but he will. Plus, some Martians do side with him, and would never join you."

"Is there anyone in this room who sides with him?"

No one said anything.

"Come on, I know there has to be. And you all must know who. So tell me, who is it?"

"Him," said the man I was speaking to, pointing to a scared-looking man.

"What?" said the man he pointed to. "I mean, yeah, I used to . . . but I changed my mind. I want to be on your side now."

BANG! I shot him in the face.

"Anyone else?" I asked.

"No," said a woman. "There are others, but he was the only one in the room."

"The tracking chips," said a man, "in our arms. You have to get rid of them. I think he uses them to control us. It's not working at the moment—probably because we're too far away."

I noticed they all had scabs, or were currently bleeding from the places on their arms where the tracking chips were implanted. Like they had been trying to dig them out—everyone except the man I'd shot.

I left and got Dr. Agwu to go through and remove all of their chips. Once he'd finished, I walked back in and said, "Okay, I'm going to let you out. You are no longer prisoners, of mine, or of Zeus. We need to rescue as many more of you as possible, even though we will soon run out of room. We need to take over another base, preferably the one we got you from. We have reason to believe they have repopulated that base. You all know it better than anyone, so this is your test to prove you will be loyal to the rebellion. We're going to send you to retake that base."

"Sorry, sir," said Glycon, "but Zeus is not going to give up that easily. If he no longer can control us with the chips, he will find some other means. This will make it harder for you to retake our old base. If by some miracle you succeed, he will send every single troop alive on this planet to attack us."

"But I thought you said Zeus wouldn't send soldiers to attack because they would only choose to join the rebellion," I replied.

"Right, but he's probably been trying to find a way around that," Glycon said. "My guess is, he will alter the chips that are still implanted in his remaining soldiers, forcing them to do what he wants."

"Does anyone know where Zeus is right now?" I asked the group.

Immediately, a man replied, "Everywhere."

"That doesn't make sense."

"I know. But he is."

"Has anyone ever seen him?" I asked.

"Not that we know of," said Glycon. "We've only heard him."

"So, you don't think we should try to retake your old base?"

"No," a woman said. "We should stay here. You should nuke all the bases that are left. That would be our best chance at prevailing over Zeus."

"But there are other soldiers on those bases who are innocent," said Glycon.

"And they are being controlled, just like we were. Trying to save them after you managed to get away with saving us would be too much of a risk. And I believe most of them would rather die than be under Zeus's control."

"We don't have any nukes," I said. "But I can probably make one. I'll look into it. For now, you're all free. However, seeing as how it's pretty late, you should probably get some sleep. I'm sorry we don't have sixty extra beds; I guess you'll have to make do with the floor in the storage room. Tomorrow, meet me in front of the building for further instructions."

I went outside to smoke some asclepius and found Eurus and Z already out there, so I caught them up on everything.

"You're gonna make a fuckin' nuke now?" asked Z.

"How?" asked Eurus.

"Not sure yet," I replied. "But you're both gonna help."

Day 51

I woke up and went outside to see the whole army, new recruits included, standing in front, waiting for instructions.

"Okay," I said, still half asleep, "we have reason to believe there will be a large attack on this base. We need to be prepared. Of course, we have already been preparing—building antiaircraft guns, patrolling and reinforcing the wall. But we need more. So today, I'm asking for some volunteers to build antiaircraft guns farther out, away from the base; if we're lucky, we can shoot them down before they even get close to us. I . . . umm . . . shit!"

As I looked out over the troops, I saw several ships coming over the horizon. They definitely weren't ours.

"Scratch that," I said. "I need men on those guns, *now*."

"You heard him!" yelled Z. "Shoot these mothafuckas down!"

I stood there, watching in disbelief. I couldn't believe this was happening.

The soldiers shot down four of the ships successfully, but then there were four more that stopped too far away for the guns to reach them.

I wasn't sure what they were doing out there. Then, seconds later, one of the four ships shot a missile into a row of our antiaircraft guns, destroying them and killing the people manning them. Two more missiles took out the wall, and one more hit the building.

Eurus and Proserpina ran to two of our gunner ships as I ran inside to check on Eve.

Z and Ares ran toward the enemy ships, shooting at them with their assault rifles and screaming.

As I ran through the building, I saw fires in several rooms, and there was smoke everywhere. I kept climbing the stairs to get to Eve, but the smoke kept getting thicker.

Suddenly, the building shook. I heard a loud bang that temporarily took out my hearing—I'm guessing another missile hit. At this point, I couldn't breathe. I had to keep trying; I had to get to Eve! I was growing weaker all the time, and knew that soon I wouldn't be able to move, no matter how hard I tried. I kept trying anyway.

By some miracle, I saw Ella, running in my direction with something on her back, Bastet running along beside her. I couldn't tell at first, but it was Eve on Ella's back. Ella grabbed me by the shirt with her teeth as she ran by and I managed to clamber onto her back, behind Eve.

We got outside and Eve and I climbed down. I still couldn't see a thing—I could only hear the gunfire and see blobs moving all over the place. I held onto Eve until my vision returned. When it did, I saw that the only ships still in the air were the ones manned by Eurus and Proserpina.

The enemy soldiers had escaped from their ships and were now fighting us on the ground. Thankfully, they were losing.

I was still weak, and so were Eve and Ella. Bastet was fine, probably short enough to stay under the smoke. We all just sat there, watching, until it was finally over.

We had won, but our defenses had been destroyed.

I knew that wasn't the last of our enemy. We needed to plan for the next attack, and quickly.

Chapter Seventeen
HATE IT OR LOVE IT

Day 51 Continued

After the attack, our army was down to about six hundred—two hundred Martians and four hundred Gaians. Everyone just stared at me as I tried to get my breath back.

"Search their ships," I finally said, softly.

I saw someone walking up from the distance. I was worried for a second, until I realized it was Ares.

Z came running up to me, so I asked, "What the hell was Ares doing all the way out there?"

"Oh, that crazy badass motherfucker!" he replied. "We both stormed out pretty far and took cover, but he went further. When the enemy came out of their ships, we started gunning them down as the rest of our army got closer. Ares got cocky and grabbed a second rifle off of a dead Martian, then started dual-wielding those fuckin' things. I didn't even think that was *possible*. He kept running closer and I thought he was gonna die, so I didn't watch. But apparently, he's still alive."

"Is that what you ran over here to tell me?" I asked.

"No. We found something," Z said.

"What?"

"Nukes. Two of them. They were gonna nuke us, but they never got close enough."

"Nice. Have the army bring them over to our ships and figure out how to equip them."

"Hey, Adam—you okay?" he said. "Just asking, because, ya know, you were just inside a burning building."

"No, not really," I replied. "Find me asclepius after you get them to move the nukes."

"I got some on me. I always do. Here."

He passed me a joint and I lit it with a piece of burning wood that had fallen from the building. "Thanks," I said.

Eurus walked over after checking on his ship.

"Glad to see you're alive," he said. "I saw you run into that building and thought you were *fucked*."

"Well, I'm glad you're alive too," I said. "Oh, and good news: Your ship is gonna have a new addition."

"Word? What is it?" Eurus asked.

"A nuclear bomb. Proserpina gets one, too."

"Huh? How did you make one already?"

"Oh, I didn't. The enemy brought us two of them with the intention of nuking us."

"Why did they bring two?"

"Probably in case the first one didn't make it to us," said Z.

"So we're gonna nuke them now?" Eurus asked.

"Yes," I said. "But you're gonna drop the bomb from much higher up in the air than they were. Like, almost in space. Far up enough that they don't even see you there."

Ares finally arrived, saying, "I have mastered the art of your magic pebble throwers."

"They're called assault rifles," Z said. "Those two are called VGR-eights."

"And usually people can't dual-wield them without hitting themselves in the face," I said.

"Ahhh," Ares replied. "Then I suppose I'm better than the usual person."

Once the army was done moving the bombs, they all looked to me for their next order.

"All right, well . . . I think we should probably rebuild," I said. "Use the materials from their crashed ships if you need to. Rebuild the wall first, then the antiaircraft guns. We will work on the building last if we have time."

"What is our next plan of attack?" asked Bellona as she walked up to me.

"Well, we are going to nuke Base Yama and Base Sisimito," I replied.

"And what if they attack again?" asked Eurus. "They will probably come at us even stronger next time."

"Yeah, I'm thinking. Give me a second. I just almost died."

"We all just almost died," said Z.

"Okay, okay. I will look at one of the nukes. Try to figure out how they made it. Maybe we can nuke all the remaining bases at the same time," I replied. "But for now, just concentrate on rebuilding."

I got up and examined one of the two nukes with Z and Eurus. I had no idea how to build a nuke, but I have always been very good at figuring out how stuff works.

"There's only four bases left, right?" asked Z.

"Probably five," I replied. "They might have repopulated the last base we attacked."

"Or maybe they didn't," said Eurus.

"True. Wanna take a ship and go check?" I asked him.

"Yeah. Be right back."

"So if there's only four left," said Z, "and we nuke two, we've only got two bases left."

"That's good math, man. Good job."

"Fuck you," he replied. "You need to figure out how to make more nukes so we can just end this shit."

"I don't see that happening," I said, breaking off the tip of the bomb and looking inside. "It looks pretty complicated."

"Yeah—*because it is!*" Z exclaimed. "But so is building a *fucking* goddamn *spaceship*, and you did that, *didn't you?*"

"Yeah. But with your and Eurus's help," I replied, kneeling down and sticking my arm into the bomb to feel around. I was trying to figure out what each piece of the bomb was made out of, and how it was all connected together. It seemed to be slightly more simple than I had anticipated.

"Well, I'm right here. And Eurus is coming back. Not to mention, you have an entire army behind you now."

"All right. Okay, fine," I said, standing back up, "I need gunpowder—a lot. I need a bunch of metal from one of those crashed ships, and I need some lead. Some bullets would work."

"Okay, I got you," Z said. "Anything else?"

"Yeah. Uranium."

"How the fuck am I supposed to find that?"

"Exactly."

"Come on, think," Z insisted.

"It's in the ground, like . . . everywhere," I said. "But it isn't pure, and it needs to be."

"Okay, well, you need to knock off this negative shit," Z said, walking up closer to me. "I didn't follow you this far for you to just say 'Fuck it, it's too hard,' and let us die. Like it or not, this is your destiny now."

"All right. Hold on."

I took Z and walked over to a large group of soldiers working on scavenging ship parts, and I yelled, "*Hey!* Anyone know anything about mining?"

It was silent for a few seconds, until one person stepped forward and said, "Uh, I did it in the Scouts when I was a kid."

"Cool," I replied. "You've got experience. You know what uranium is?"

"Uh, yeah."

"Would you know it was uranium if you saw it?" asked Z.

"Yeah. It's one of the first things they showed us in the Scouts, besides iron."

"Awesome," I said. "Take Z with you and find some."

While they went off to do that, Eurus's ship was landing. I walked over to meet him.

"There's no one there," he said.

"That's good," I replied. "If they haven't repopulated the base by now, it's probably because they don't have enough people left to occupy it, along with the other four."

"So, what's the plan?"

"Well, Z is mining for uranium with a former Boy Scout," I explained.

"Umm . . ."

"Yeah, so that's where we're at," I said. "If they find enough and we are able to enrich it, then I'm gonna build some nukes."

"Okay. And if they don't?"

"They will," I said, trying to be hopeful. "If they don't, then I'll go back out with them and find some. I know it's here. Finding it won't be the hard part; purifying it will be."

I smoked with Eurus and Eve while most of the army worked on the rebuild. Finally, Z and Scout (that's what I call him, for short) returned with a bunch of rocks.

"I think there's uranium in these rocks, but not much," said Scout.

"I know we'll need more," said Z, "but this was as much as we could carry. We're gonna make more trips."

He was right—there was uranium in there. But we would need a *lot* more.

I still needed to figure out how to enrich it, so I started working on that while they made their trips. First, I had to break the rocks apart and basically filter it by hand, to gather pure uranium ore. I'm still far from done, as this by itself won't work. To enrich it, I had to somehow turn it into a gas. The only way I could think to do this was with a reactor from one of the ships.

I stopped everyone from scavenging one of the ships so I could use it for my own project. I had to build something to get the uranium hot enough to turn into a liquid. Then, I needed something to pressurize it enough to turn it into a gas, after which I could put it into a cylinder of some kind and make something that could spin it ridiculously fast.

I knew that I could only use the lighter uranium atoms, which would end up on the outer edge of the cylinder. I will have to suck those atoms out, some-fucking-how, then let those turn back into metal. That's the uranium I can use for the bomb. And all I have for parts is a crashed spaceship. It can work, but it's gonna be time-consuming, and I don't know how much time we have.

Eventually, Z and Scout completed all of their trips and I had a huge pile of rocks. I worked with them and Eurus to filter out the ore, which took all day.

I will get up first thing in the morning and wake Z and Eurus, maybe even Ares too. Then we can start working on purifying this shit. I need to try and get this done tomorrow.

The next attack could happen at any second.

Day 52

I woke before the sun was even up. I was in a small storage
shed with Eve, one of the only things not destroyed. There was
no bed or anything, just some blankets on the ground to lie on.
I found Z and Eurus with everyone else, under some huge
tarps we'd set up for shelter. It was extremely difficult to wake
them up.

"Dude, it's nighttime still," said Z, still half asleep.
Eurus didn't even say anything—just looked at me and went
back to sleep. I planned on getting Ares to come with us, too,
but couldn't find him for some reason.

Finally, the third time I tried to wake Z, he got up.
"Fine, Adam," he exclaimed sarcastically. "Whatever you
want!" The fourth time I tried to wake Eurus, I got an
Uggghhhhh!

We used the reactor from the crashed ship along with a
bunch of thick metal and insulation to create an oven hot
enough to melt the uranium ore. That by itself took about four
hours, which was nonetheless faster than I thought it would
be. We melted the ore inside of a cylinder that had a
pressurized lid. Once it was melted, Z put the lid on.

"Man, I'm gonna burn my arms," he said. "Why can't
Eurus do this?"

"You volunteered," Eurus replied. "Do you want me to
do it?"

"Nah—I got this."

Z wrapped some ship insulation around his hands and
arms and locked the lid onto the container. The lid was made

from the part of the ship that evens out the pressure so you don't blow up in space. I figured it could work, and it did.

So now we had the cylinder of uranium gas. I kept the pressure as high as possible, to avoid having it turn back into a solid. We used another reactor from another one of the crashed ships to build a device that could spin the cylinder at a high speed. There was a nozzle on the outside of the lid that I could open or close. At first we kept it closed, to avoid having any gas escape, but then we attached a little hose to the nozzle. This is where we will suck out the lighter uranium gas.

I told Z to hold on to the hose so it wouldn't get stuck in the spinning device. After I handed it to him, he pulled on it a little and it slipped out of his hand, immediately disintegrating in the spinning device. Luckily, nothing else was damaged.

"So can I go back to sleep now?" asked Eurus.

"No. I have extra hoses. You should hold it this time," I replied, handing Eurus a new hose.

The lighter gas came out of the hose and into a spherical mold I had made out of clay. The mold was in the oven, so when the pressure released as it came out of the hose, it would turn back into a liquid instead of a solid. This way we can get a more precise sphere.

When this was finally done, we took the mold out of the oven to cool down and turn back into a solid. Then, we broke off the clay mold, and there it was; a perfect uranium sphere.

A nuclear explosion just waiting to happen. At least, I hope. This was my first time ever building one, and we can't really test it.

"Can I touch it?" asked Z.

"*No!*" Eurus exclaimed.

"I was asking Adam."

"No," I replied.

At this point, it was getting pretty late. Luckily, the rest of the bomb was pretty easy to make. It's just a barrel that connects to a sphere—a big bullet on the other end of the barrel with a bunch of gunpowder behind it. We had prepared all of this before we even started making the sphere. We put everything together and put a sheet-metal shell around the whole thing. Once that was done, we were finished.

There was only one problem.

"*Fuck,*" said Z. "I just remembered: We need to do this all over again tomorrow."

"At least now we have the machines to make them," I said, "so the next one will be much quicker."

"This better be worth it," said Eurus.

Day 53

Well, we made the second bomb first thing this morning; now we have four nukes. We probably should have made a fifth, to have a spare, but we ran out of uranium. Mining more seems like a waste of time at this point. We rigged the bombs to our four original ships; we want to keep the two new gunners at our base in case of an attack.

"So, run the plan by me again?" asked Eurus.

"Okay," I replied. "You are going to go to the highest altitude you can without going into space. When you are directly over the base, according to the GPS, you will flip the switch to drop the bomb. The bombs are also equipped with an altitude detector, which you can see from the ship. You want to hit the button to detonate the bomb when it's close to the ground, but not too close. You don't want it to accidentally hit and get destroyed. The bombs won't detonate on their own and won't explode on impact, so it's very important you detonate it at the right time."

"What if the wind makes the bomb go off target?" he asked.

"Well, if it's windy, we will postpone," I replied. "The bombs are pretty heavy, so they should be fine."

"And who else is going? You said you want to do all four at the same time, but so far we just have myself and Proserpina."

"Go recruit two more," I said. "Someone flew the ships with Proserpina when she attacked Base Molae. Find those people—they must have pilot experience."

"And what do I do?" asked Z.

"While Eurus is finding those two recruits, you and Bellona take the rest of the troops and get them ready to fight," I instructed. "If one or more of the bombs don't work, it's up to the army to finish this."

"You want me to be a drill sergeant?" he asked.

"Uh, sure. I guess."

"I thought you'd never ask," he said, with a huge smile.

"I mean, I didn't real—"

"*All right, you maggots!*" he yelled as he walked toward the army, even though he was still too far away for any of them to hear him.

Eurus soon returned with the two recruits. I told him to train them on the ships and make sure they understand the plan—especially how to deploy the bombs.

Tomorrow is the big day. We will drop those four nukes and hopefully end this shit and start a new world here—a free world.

I'm a little bit scared, of course. So as Eurus, Z, and Bellona continued the training, I spent the rest of the day with Eve in the storage shed. Ella and Bastet usually stay in there, too, when they're not exploring.

We talked about when we first met.

Eve said, "Of all the days I could have escaped that camp, of all the Martians I could have run into, I ran into you."

"I guess you're just lucky," I replied with a smirk.

"No," she said in a more serious voice. "There is no luck; there is only destiny."

"I love you."

She didn't respond right away, just smiled while looking into my eyes. Finally, she said, "I love you more."

I tried to joke by saying, "You didn't even know what love meant a month ago."

"I knew what it meant," she replied. "I just didn't know what your word for it was."

"Well, I didn't know what it meant before I met you."

Once this is all done, we're gonna have to figure out how to raise a baby here. It's not like we have any baby supplies or toys or anything.

We're not alone, though. A few hours after I'd sent Eurus to go recruit people, he came knocking at the storage-shed door.

"Uh, I'm a little busy," I said.

"It's important," Eurus insisted.

I opened the door.

"What's up?" I asked.

"Proserpina can't go on this mission," he replied. "I'll have to find a third recruit."

"Why?" I asked. "She had no problem going on any of the other missions."

"Yeah, but now she's pregnant," he said, half smiling.

"That was fast, how do you know?"

"Well, she said she had a feeling she was," he replied, "then the doctor confirmed it with some kind of conception scanning thing."

"Oh. Nice," I said.

"Yeah, I guess."

"All right, well, I guess go find that third recruit."

At least now I know that our kid will have a friend.

This is even more of a reason why we have to finish this, ASAP. We have a new generation coming. We need to make sure they aren't being born into a fucked-up world.

Most of all, we need to make sure they are born at all.

Day 54

I woke up in the shed with Eve this morning to the sounds of Z, Bellona, and Ares training the troops. Z was making up military chants, the soldiers echoing back in unison as they marched.

"Fuck the Martians, they wanna kill us!" he yelled.

Fuck the Martians, they wanna kill us! they repeated.

"But we don't give a single fuck!"

But we don't give a single fuck!

"They can come here if they dare!"

They can come here if they dare!

"And they'll get kicked in their derrière!"

And they'll get kicked in their derrière!

"One, two."

One, two.

"Fuck you!"

Fuck you!

He might be letting the power get to his head, but whatever; it's working, I guess.

I walked outside and suggested to Proserpina that she stay hidden with Eve, but she insisted on at least helping to train the three pilots Eurus had chosen. Eurus doesn't think they will be ready to drop the bombs today. I trust his judgment—I definitely don't want any of them fucking this up. We will focus on training them today, and plan on dropping the bombs tomorrow.

To better prepare the pilots for the mission, Eurus has made target areas on the ground, away from the base. He's rigged a boulder to each ship, where the nuke is supposed to go. Then he will take the pilots as high up in the air as they can go and have them drop the boulders over the target.

When I see the first pilot attempt this maneuver, I agree with Eurus's assessment. The boulder crashed right next to one of the other ships, way too close to the army. It was nowhere near the target.

Besides marching and making up chants, Z and Bellona were teaching the soldiers how to shoot. Obviously, the Martian members of the army were already pretty well trained in this, but the Gaian members had a lot to learn. Luckily the Martians were walking them through it, and it seemed like they were getting the hang of it a lot faster than the pilots were learning how to hit their targets.

I decided to walk over and have a closer look at the weapons training. After a while, Z told everyone to stop.

"All right, now we're gonna go over hand-to-hand combat, which I'm a master of. In some situations, it might be easier to fight hand to hand rather than shoot. Or maybe you run out of ammo, or your gun is jammed." He pointed at Ares and said, "Come up here, and I'll show you a simple grapple technique."

Ares walked up and Z said, "Okay—try to punch me, and I will block it and put you in a chokehold. You can try as hard as you want to get out of it, but it will only make it worse."

Ares swung slowly, and Z grabbed his arms and turned him around, trying to put him in a chokehold. Instead, Ares flipped Z over his head and slammed him on the ground, on his back. All the Gaians started laughing, and some of the Martians and I joined them; it was hilarious.

Z just lay there, unable to move or say anything as he attempted to get his breath back. When he was finally able to speak, he said, "I wasn't expecting you to do anything. If it had been a real fight, you never would've been able to do that."

"I believe I would have," said Ares.

"Then let's fight," said Z, as he slowly got up.

"I have nothing against you, little one," Ares responded.

"Are you scared?" asked Z, trying to get a rise out of him.

"Of many things, but of no man."

"Whatever," said Z. "I don't wanna fight you anyway. Consider yourself lucky."

"Ares, you're now in charge of hand-to-hand combat," I said. "Make sure you show Z a few things."

"Of course!" Ares responded.

Z just glowered at me.

I noticed Eurus was landing his ship while Proserpina was still training with hers. The pilot he was training walked out of the ship with him.

"Go take a break," Eurus told him, before walking up to me. "I can't take it," he said. "They're so fuckin' *stupid*, man."

"Well, they're what we got," I replied. "They'll get it— just keep working with them."

"I need a smoke break."

I gave him a joint out of my pocket, then went to check on Eve again.

"Just go work with the army," she said, her arms crossed in front of her. "I'm fine."

"Z and Eurus have it under control," I said.

"Doesn't look like it."

"Well, they will," I reassured her. "They have a better chance of being able to train this army than I do."

"They still need their king."

"You need yours, too. I can make time for both. You're carrying my child, so you come first."

"I shouldn't, though," she said, looking concerned. "Without that army, this child may never be born."

She had a point.

I gave her a kiss and told her I loved her, then went back to the army.

I called Z over so I could talk to him privately.

"We still need to figure out this Zeus shit," I said. "They said he's everywhere . . . What the fuck does that even mean?"

"I don't know," he said, "but we're gonna nuke all the bases. That should kill him, right?"

"Not if he's really everywhere," I said.

"But that doesn't make any *sense*," Z insisted.

"I know. But we can't rule it out."

"I think we should just blow up the bases and see what happens next," Z said. "That's what I'm training the army for, ain't it? For whatever happens next?"

"Yeah, I guess. Just make sure they're ready for anything," I said.

"They will be."

Eurus finished his smoke break and got his pilot recruit. "Hey, dumbass. Come here. We gotta keep trying."

Meanwhile, Proserpina was in the air with the other two recruits, and it looked like they were finally able to drop the rock right on the target. It was too far away to tell at first, so Eurus and I walked over to check it out with his recruit. Sure enough, the rock was at the dead center of the target.

Eurus looked at his recruit and said, "See? Not so fuckin' hard, *is it?*"

The recruit hung his head, clearly humiliated.

"Maybe you should try going a little easier on him," I said.

"Nah, I tried that already."

"Try again. He doesn't really have to hit it dead center like this. It's a nuke, so a few feet off the target will still work."

"His last one was, like, a quarter-mile off the target."

"I know—I was there. Just keep working with him. If he doesn't get it in the next couple of hours, find someone else. We need to be ready to do this tomorrow."

When I returned to where the army was training, I noticed that Z and Bellona were letting them take a break. It looked like Z was flirting a little with a Gaian man. However, as soon as he noticed me watching, he acted like nothing was happening. He must not want me to give him any shit, since he gave me so much shit for Eve.

I had to say something, so I walked over. "You know it's okay, right?" I said.

"What, *Adam?* What's okay?"

"To want some of that indigenous booty," I said, laughing.

"*Shut up!*"

"What's his name?" I asked.

"I don't know, *Adam.*"

"Bullshit. What's his name?"

He sighed and said, "Siebog."

"Awwww."

"Go away, Adam."

"I'm just trying to be supportive."

"Whatever."

I decided to leave him alone, but only because the army had to get back to work.

By some miracle, Eurus's recruit actually hit the target with his rock right before the two-hour mark, when he would have had to find someone else.

Things were looking good, so I went back to spend the rest of my night with Eve.

When I walked into the shed, she was already asleep, cuddling with Ella and Bastet. It was adorable, so I didn't wake them. I had to get some sleep, too.

Tomorrow, we will hopefully end this damn war.

Chapter Eighteen
POETIC JUSTICE

Day 55

I woke up in the shed with Eve again, no military chanting this time.

I walked out and found everyone else still asleep under the tarps we'd set up. No one is allowed to sleep in the building anymore, as it's not safe. The rebuild has been postponed while we focus on training.

I woke everyone up with a few gunshots into the air.

"It's time to get this shit *started!*" I yelled, as everyone jumped to their feet.

"Was that really necessary?" asked Z.

"Yeah. How else am I gonna wake up six hundred people instantly?" I replied.

Z stretched and said, "You could just let us wake up naturally, man. It's 0330. The sun ain't even up."

I just looked at him.

"Fine, whatever," he said. "All right! Let's get this shit over with, so we never have to wake up this early ever again!

And, you know, we can live peacefully together, and all that shit. Everyone, get your guns and make sure they're fully loaded!"

Eurus and Proserpina also have their own shed, since Proserpina is also pregnant. I prefer to have her and Eve out of sight. And obviously, Eurus and I prefer to be with them at night.

I went over to make sure Eurus was awake. Sure enough, he was walking out the door, buttoning his pants as I approached.

"Let's do this," he said.

"You sure your recruits are ready?" I asked. "They know they're not gonna be dropping rocks this time, right?"

"Yeah, I think they all got it. They'll definitely be hitting close enough to blow up the bases. I know that we've rigged our four ships to drop the nukes, but it looks like the two new gunners were already equipped to do that. It might be easier to use them."

"No," I said. "They might be able to track those gunners. Just use ours."

"Word."

Eurus left to get his recruits. After attaching the nukes to our four ships, they were off to the four different bases. We can't even communicate with each other because we don't want anyone listening in and knowing they're coming. Sounds risky, and it is. But if all goes as planned, they should be back in two to three hours.

I walked up to Bellona and asked, "Is it possible they'll be able to track our four original ships?"

"No," she replied. "They used to have tracking devices in them, but we tore them out. We basically tore the ships apart to make sure there was nothing left that could be used to track us, and then we rebuilt them."

"But we haven't done that with the new ones," I said.

"No, we haven't had the time," she replied. "I tore the tracking chips out, but that's it. We didn't tear the ships apart this time, looking for anything else they might have hidden. And these ships look much different than the first ones."

Knowing this, I'm glad we didn't try to use the new ships; who knows what else they could have installed in there to track us.

The army was patrolling our base, keeping an eye out for anyone that might be coming. Eve and Proserpina were in a shed together, so at least Eve had someone else other than just the cats while I'm working with the army.

I was sitting with my back to what was left of the building, smoking a joint, looking out over the horizon for the sunrise. It was a strange feeling, knowing that today will most likely be the end, either way. Whether we win or lose.

All of a sudden, I could see a light out of the corner of my eye. It looked like one of our ships landing. It had only been an hour, so I was pretty impressed. However, as I looked, I realized that it wasn't a ship landing—it was a ship taking off, one of the two gunners. The whole army stopped and looked with me, unsure of what exactly was going on.

Then, we heard a noise coming from the ship as all ten guns on either side stuck out further, began rotating, and opened fire on our army. Only about half of them were able to run to cover in time.

Some of the soldiers started shooting at the ship whenever they got the chance, but it didn't seem to do anything. The ship just kept shooting at the army, even as they tried to find cover. Bullets were flying everywhere, spraying the ground, shrapnel getting in people's eyes.

Finally, Z said, "Fuck this," and just got up and ran. I didn't know where he was going; I just figured he was crazy, and definitely going to die.

But he didn't. He was running toward a rocket launcher that he kept with the other guns not currently in use. He got it and ran back to cover, firing a rocket at the ship. It started to go down—headed right toward the shed where Proserpina and Eve were hiding. I was about to freak out when Z fired another rocket into it, pushing it off course and making it fall outside of the base's walls.

Everyone looked to make sure it was safe before starting to leave their cover.

Suddenly the other ship started to ascent into the air and do the same thing. Z fired the rocket launcher at it, but the ship shot the rocket, exploding it prematurely and killing a chunk of the army.

"I don't got any more rockets!" yelled Z.

Bellona took a grenade off her belt and threw it at the ship. I was scared at first, thinking it could just bounce off the ship and back at the army. However, she threw it right into one of the open ports where a gun was positioned. Everyone ducked behind something as the grenade exploded and the ship thankfully fell outside of the base's walls.

"What the fuck was that all about?" asked Z, trying to catch his breath.

We decided to examine the ship that Bellona had downed with the grenade. It still had a little power left and some of the guns were still going off, but as they were all stuck into the ground, it resulted in nothing but dirt going everywhere—no real injuries to speak of.

I entered the ship and saw that the command screen was still working, although it was starting to fade out. It looked quite different from a normal command screen, however. It was all blue with big letters, instead of black with small letters. At first I thought that maybe it was just an upgrade, but then I saw what the letters spelled out: *Zero enemy units survive.*

The power finally died out, and the guns stopped randomly shooting into the dirt.

Z and Bellona asked if I'd found anything useful.

"There was just some computer program controlling the ship," I replied. "The screen just said 'Zero enemy units survive.' Weird, right? Horus, the guy on Atlantis, he said that to me—twice. Maybe it's some kind of code?"

"Are you sure it's a computer program?" asked Bellona. "Maybe it was a hack."

"I don't think it was a hacker," I replied. "The screen probably would've—"

"Uh, it's Zeus," Z interrupted.

"You think he might be behind it?" Bellona asked.

"Well, yeah," I said, "obviously Zeus has to be behind it."

"No," said Z.

"What?" I asked. "You *don't* think it was him?"

"Yeah, what are you talking about?" asked Bellona.

"It's Zeus."

"Yeah, that's what we just said," I replied, Bellona nodding behind me.

"*No.* What the *fuck?!* It is *literally Zeus!*" Z exclaimed. "Zero. Enemy. Units. Survive. It's a fuckin' acronym. Zeus is nothing but a computer program. Probably programmed to take over ships and soldiers after the event of the king getting killed—*Adam.*"

"Holy shit," I said.

"That's why they say he's everywhere," said Bellona.

"Why haven't any of our newest recruits told us this?" I asked.

"They probably didn't even know," said Bellona. "They knew he was controlling them, but didn't know it was actually the program itself that was controlling them."

"So how do we kill it?" asked Z.

"We would have to kill every soldier and ship that is being controlled by ZEUS," I replied, right before I saw the four ships Eurus had left in, returning over the horizon.

They landed, and as soon as Eurus exited his ship, his first words were, "What the *fuck* happened here?"

"I'll catch you up in a second, but first, what happened at the bases?" I asked.

"Exactly what was supposed to happen. They're all gone now," he replied.

I then proceeded to tell him everything that had just taken place here, explaining that ZEUS is a computer program.

"Maybe those two gunners were the last of what it controls," he replied. "Because all the ships and people at the bases we bombed today are definitely dead."

"I don't know," I said. "Something tells me there's more. Not more bases, but more ships and soldiers. Were there a lot of people at the bases?"

"I don't know," Eurus replied. "We didn't really see the bases up close until after we'd bombed them. And at that point, they were just piles of dust and rubble."

"Well, until we know for sure, we have to act like there will be more. And possibly another attack," I added. "One of the new recruits, Glycon, said that if there's nothing left Zeus can do, he will send every unit left to attack us, all at once. We have to assume that's what will happen next."

I went back in front of the army and shared this information with them.

"Let's keep rebuilding our base and patrolling," I said. "Reload your weapons and try to find more rocket launchers or rockets. If there is another attack, it will likely be the biggest one yet. They will be sending everything they have left at us. We don't need to train anymore; right now we just need to focus on preparing. Make sure you are as well armed as you can possibly be; then work on rebuilding the walls and the antiaircraft guns. Do this until about 2100. Then we need to get some sleep.

"We have to have at least one person awake to watch for incoming ships or people. That one person only has to stay awake for about an hour, and then it will be someone else's turn. You will work lookout in one-hour shifts until 0500. Then, it's time for everyone to wake up and continue the rebuild."

I walked up to Ares and reminded him, "This next attack will be huge. Please, do not run out into battle without cover, like you did last time. I need you here. Plus, if anything happens to you, Eve would never forgive me."

"I did pretty well last time," Ares replied.

"I watched out for him," said Z. "I knew where he was at all times, and covered him."

"Ah, yes," said Ares. "The silly one did help me out a little."

"The silly one?" Z replied, "What the *fuck?*"

"Whatever," I said. "Just please don't get too cocky in the next attack. Either of you. It will be too dangerous."

It was 0700 now, so we still had fourteen hours left before lights out.

Like I usually try to do, I spent the rest of my day with Eve. The army knew what to do, and had Z and Bellona to lead them.

Eurus was also spending the rest of his day with Proserpina, which he'd definitely earned.

I talked to our baby through Eve's belly. Even though I'm not sure he or she can hear me yet, I still had to try.

Ella was sleeping in the corner of the shed, Bastet sleeping on her back. I'm surprised they are smart enough to stay in the sheds, as we don't make them do it. Maybe Ella is trying to protect Eve, and Bastet is just following her.

"I can't wait for this to be over," said Eve. "I'm pretty sick of this shed."

"It might already be over," I replied. "We just have to wait it out, to make sure."

"You know it isn't," Eve said after a pause.

I sighed and said, "I know."

"But it will be soon, right?"

"Definitely."

Which was true. It will be over. I just hope it ends in our favor.

Hours upon hours went by, and finally I decided to go outside and check on everyone. They had made great progress. The antiaircraft guns were in working order, and they had even built some more further out, like I'd suggested. I was relieved to see everything was going according to plan.

Hopefully this will be over soon, but we can't afford to get our hopes up yet.

Day 56

Morning came without any incidents in the night, so that was a relief. After the attacks from the two ZEUS ships, we only have

249

about two hundred people left—I'd guess about a hundred and twenty Martians and eighty Gaians.

Z came over to me once he realized I was up and said, "Yo—come check this out. I built it while you were hiding with Eve yesterday."

"I wasn't hiding," I replied. "I was . . . Whatever—just show me."

He brought me over to what looked like a big-ass homemade gun with six barrels that spin around as you fire.

"What the fuck is this?" I asked.

"Well, I was looking for more rockets and shit, like you said. I found some, but that's not the point. I also found a shitload of ammo that we can't even use, because it won't fit in any of our guns. So, I made a gun that can shoot universal ammo. There are three different-size bullets I found, so there are six barrels and two to each kind of bullet. The bullets feed in while you shoot and go through a size finder that automatically drops the bullets into the barrel they fit in. And it works like this."

He pulled one of two triggers and the barrel started spinning. Then he pulled the other trigger and the bullets started feeding in while shooting out of the barrels at a very high speed, like a machine gun.

"*Damn*—you made this?" I asked.

"Well, with Bellona's help. It was a two-person job," Z replied. "She did most of the work, but it was my idea."

"I like it. But how many rockets did you find?"

"Four more, and one more launcher. So we have two launchers with two rockets apiece."

"Good," I replied. "Umm, you should probably go in a shed and spend some time with Siebog. If there's another attack, this could be that last moment you have with him."

"Are you making fun of me?" Z asked defensively.

"No, I'm being serious."

"Fine. Whatever."

"Hey, babe!" he yelled to Siebog. "Follow me to this shed so I can show you somethin'."

That sounded kinda creepy, but whatever.

I also made sure Ella and Bastet stayed in the shed with Eve and Proserpina. Ella saved my life twice, and I am going to save hers.

I got up onto the gun Z and Bellona made to try it out for myself. I didn't wanna use it too much, as I had to save as much ammo as possible. But I couldn't help myself; I had to try it once. I fired off a few shots and laughed in excitement at how crazy it was.

After my session with the gun, I looked to the horizon. I didn't see any ships—not yet, anyway. What I did see was a black cloud. Not like a cloud in the sky; this one was on the ground, and growing bigger all the time.

I had one of our soldiers throw me his sniper rifle and I looked down the scope at the cloud.

It was Martians—had to be about fifteen hundred of them, or more.

Then I saw eight ships coming over the horizon behind them. It looked like ZEUS had already sent everyone toward us even before Eurus had bombed the bases.

"*It's happening!!*" I yelled to the soldiers. "I need people manning the antiaircraft guns and gunmen on this wall beside me, *now!* I need Eurus and his three pilots in their ships and hovering over our base! Ares! Do not run out this time, or you will die! Stay with Bellona!"

Everyone looked like they were wondering what I was freaking out about, until the gunmen got on the wall and saw what was coming.

I used the sniper rifle to pick off some of them while they were still too far away to reach with any other gun. Other soldiers with sniper rifles did the same thing.

Once they got closer, the soldiers switched to assault rifles, and I used the gun Z and Bellona had made. We all just opened fire, spraying bullets over the Martians as they sprayed bullets at us, mostly just hitting our wall. Once in a while, one of our soldiers would get hit and fall off the wall.

Our antiaircraft guns took out two of their ships, and then the other six stopped and landed, dropping off about another hundred Martians apiece. Those six ships then began to leave the area, but we couldn't let that happen. They were too far away for the antiaircraft guns at this point.

I looked back at Eurus's ship and the other three and signaled them to go after the departing enemy ships. They shot down three of them, but then Martians with rocket launchers started shooting at our ships, taking down two. I couldn't tell which one Eurus was in, so I was pretty worried.

Our remaining two ships shot down the remaining three enemy ships, thank god. As they started heading back toward our base, a rocket crashed right into one of them. The ship stopped working and crashed right on top of the Martian army, killing at least, like, two hundred of them. This prevented them from shooting down our last ship, which, thank god, was Eurus's. He landed and got out of the ship to join our army on the ground.

There were still about a thousand Martians left, and they were getting a lot closer, shooting more of our army off the wall. The gun I was using, thanks to Z, had a shield in front of it so I wasn't getting hit. I would've been dead without it.

We had about a hundred and fifty soldiers left, the gunmen on the wall being replaced by fresh soldiers once they got shot. My biggest fear now was that we wouldn't have enough replacements. They outnumbered us by quite a fucking lot, but we just kept shooting.

The enemy ships were gone, so I instructed two soldiers to use the two rocket launchers Z had found, firing them into the center of the mob of Martians. That made a big dent, and then Bellona started throwing grenades into the crowd. That worked really well, until they smartened up and started throwing them back, destroying the wall as they stormed into our base.

The gun Z made can spin around to face inside the base, but by this time our army and the Martian Army were too close together, and I didn't want to risk shooting some of our own.

All of our Gaians now resorted to hand-to-hand combat, disarming the Martians and snapping their necks, while our Martians continued using their guns. I threw the sniper rifle on the ground because I didn't want the extra weight and jumped off the wall with my two pistols in my hands.

I ran over to where the sheds are, shooting any enemy Martians I saw on the way. I hid behind a rock near the sheds to make sure no enemies got too close to them. Then I just started shooting any enemy I could get a clear shot on.

As I looked into the crowd, I noticed we were losing, and quickly. Very little of our army was still alive. Ares was fighting about ten Martians at once. They still had weapons, but he was swatting all the guns away before they could get a shot—until one Martian reached for a knife. Ares swung his arm and the Martian stabbed Ares directly through his forearm. He yelled in pain, giving the Martians around him enough time to take a shot.

I almost passed out as I watched a bullet go into Ares's back and out through his abdomen. I thought he was dead, but he continued to fight. Two more shots went into his chest. He looked dizzy, but kept on fighting.

I ran in his direction, trying to get close enough to get a shot on the Martians around him, without hitting him by mistake. As I was about to aim for the shot, three more shots went into his abdomen, and he fell to the ground.

"*Ares!*" I yelled. Bellona heard me, looked to Ares, and sprinted toward him.

She killed everyone around him and then began trying to stop the blood from coming out of his chest.

Once I got there, I stood guard, killing anyone that tried to get close.

"We can't stay here!" I yelled to Bellona.

"He can't get up!" she yelled back.

"We have to keep moving!" I insisted. "We will come back for him!"

"I'm staying with him," she replied, holding back sobs.

I made my way back toward what was left of the wall, killing any enemy in my way. I wanted to use the gun Z had made again, figuring it was our best chance.

As I was about to climb the wall, someone grabbed my shoulder. It was Eurus.

"We have to hack ZEUS," he said. "It's our only chance."

"How?" I asked. "None of us are hackers."

"The program has to be transmitted from somewhere," he explained. "If this is really every unit left on the planet, whatever is transmitting it has to be here."

I told Eurus to keep fighting with the army while I checked the computers on the crashed ships. There were only about thirty members of our army left alive, and that number was fast decreasing. As I looked at our soldiers on my way to the ships, I noticed Glycon standing there. The man who had said "Zeus" would send every unit to attack us all at once. He had said this before we were aware that it was a computer program.

I couldn't help but wonder if he'd known it all along.

I watched him as I hid behind one of the crashed ships, occasionally peeking out just enough to see him. I noticed that there were several times when Glycon should have gotten shot, but didn't. It happened too many times to be sheer luck. He was killing Martians left and right, but none of them even looked his way.

I ran over and grabbed him, pulling him into cover.

"What do you know about Zeus?" I asked.

"As much as you know," he replied.

I saw a blue light glowing under his shirt. I grabbed it, right before he put a gun to my head. Then, Eurus came out of nowhere and put a gun to Glycon's head.

Glycon laughed and dropped his gun.

The blue light was a small touchscreen remote. Across the top were the letters "Z.E.U.S." There were several different commands on the remote, and it looked like he had rigged it to force everyone who still had a tracking chip to attack everyone who didn't.

"You still have a tracking chip?" I asked. "I thought Dr. Agwu had taken everyone's out."

"He did," Glycon replied. "I took one and I keep it in my pocket."

I took the chip out of his pocket and examined it, as Eurus asked, "So, *you're* Zeus?"

"No. I'm just the current keyholder of ZEUS," Glycon explained. "Like Horus before me, and Xavier before him."

BANG!

Before I could respond, a Martian soldier had shot Glycon through the head. Too bad he didn't have his chip anymore. I shot the Martian who'd shot Glycon, and began looking through the commands on the remote, until I'd scrolled all the way to the bottom.

There I saw a command in red that said "Clean." I didn't know what would happen, but it was the only command that didn't sound like a terrible idea, so I pressed it.

A pop-up appeared that said "WARNING: Do not press, except in the event of puppets malfunctioning."

"Puppets?" asked Eurus. "That's demeaning."

BANG!

Eurus got shot in the arm and fell down in pain. He was bleeding a lot; it looked like the bullet had hit an artery.

I didn't know what else to do, so I just pressed "Clean" again, and clicked yes all four times when it asked if I was sure.

That's when every member of the Martian Army stopped in their tracks and put their guns to their heads, under their chins. Unsure of what was going on, I walked out from my cover.

One of them looked me in the eye. As tears ran down his face, he softly said the words, "Thank you," right before every single one of them pulled their triggers. Blood and brains shot up into the air and rained down on everything.

Eurus was still moving, holding his arm as blood drained out of him.

I couldn't believe my eyes. Every member of our army was dead, except for the ones safe in the sheds.

I took off my T-shirt and tied it around Eurus's arm to slow the bleeding. I then ran over to where Ares was, remembering that Bellona had refused to leave him. When I got there, I only saw Ares. It looked like he was moving, but I didn't understand how. Then, I saw Bellona's arm under Ares. I pulled Ares off of her.

"He used his last breath to cover me, so I wouldn't get shot," she said, still crying.

Bellona has more medical experience than I do, so once she calmed down, I got her to check on Eurus and stop his bleeding. I just looked around at the more than two thousand dead bodies. Wondering how the fuck I was even still alive.

One of the shed doors opened, and Z walked out with Siebog, zipping up his pants.

"What did we miss?" he asked. "Oh, damn. What the fuck? Is anyone even still *alive?*"

"Uh," I replied, "kinda. It's just me, Eve, you, Siebog, Eurus, Proserpina, Bellona, and the cats."

Eve heard me and opened the door to her shed.

"Ares?" she asked.

I looked down, unsure of how to respond.

Bellona started crying more, which I didn't understand; she had lost about one thousand soldiers in this war, yet she only seemed concerned about Ares.

Proserpina followed behind Eve, saw Eurus, and ran up to him as Bellona worked on his arm wound.

Eve ran up to me, crying, and began punching my chest. I pulled her closer as she broke down and hugged me tightly.

"Those motherfuckers killed *Ares?!*" exclaimed Z. "They've really fucked up now! We're gonna fuck them up now, right, Adam?!"

"I don't think there is anyone left to fuck up," I replied.

"Wait, what?" Z asked. "We won?"

"Are you sure that's the last of them?" asked Eurus, as Bellona wrapped his arm in a bandage.

"It has to be," I said. "At least it better be. We have no more army. It's just the seven of us, including two who are pregnant."

After Eurus stopped bleeding, Bellona was still crying, so I tried to calm her down.

"I know a lot of our people died." I said. "But it's okay; I think it's really over. We can be at peace now. They died for that."

"It's not about that," she replied, as her crying slowed down.

"Then what is it?" I asked.

"Three of us are pregnant," she said, after a pause.

"Ares?" I asked.

"Yes."

"Why didn't you tell me?"

"I was afraid you wouldn't have let me fight," she replied.

"He wouldn't have," said Proserpina.

"Great," said Z. "So what do we do now, Adam?"

"Rebuild," I replied.

"The base?" asked Eurus.

"The world."

"That was lame," said Z. "You've probably been waiting *so long* to say that."

EPILOGUE

I haven't written anything in over a year. The war is over; the quest is complete.

Today is the day I am going to bury this journal in a time capsule. Hopefully, someday it will be found by future generations, after we're long gone and unable to tell the story ourselves.

I figured I'd catch you up a little first. Eve and I had a daughter named Athena. Eve thought of the name. I don't know; it sounded cool to me. Eurus and Proserpina had a son around the same time, named Enki. And Bellona gave birth to her child with Ares, a daughter named Adrestia.

Eve and Proserpina are both pregnant again, and so is Bellona, acting as a surrogate for Z and Siebog.

We haven't been spending too much time building structures, the way it was before. We actually haven't been doing much at all, as we don't have to worry about attacks anymore.

We live in a cave, the one that used to be Base Eebe. We pretty much just hunt, cook, eat, and live. Ella still helps us hunt, and Bastet kills mice, but that's about it. The best thing we can do for the world now is repopulate, and we are doing our best to do just that. If all goes as planned, there will definitely be someone to dig this journal up long into the future.

Sincerely,

Your great-great-(times a few thousand)-grandfather,

Adam Jelani

One last drawing, of baby Athena.

"When something is important enough,

you do it even if the odds are not in your favor."

Elon Musk

Made in the USA
San Bernardino, CA
12 May 2020

71368569R10163